DRAGONFLY DANCE
A Mercy Mountain Novella

Copyright © 2020 by Becca Maxton

All rights reserved. Except for use in any review, the reproduction or utilization of this work in whole or in part in any form by any electronic, mechanical or other means, now known or hereinafter invented, including xerography, photocopying and recording, or in any information storage or retrieval system, is forbidden without the written permission of the publisher.

This is a work of fiction. Names, characters, places and incidents are either the product of the author's imagination or are used fictitiously, and any resemblance to actual persons, living or dead, business establishments, events or locales is entirely coincidental.

Printed in the USA.

Cover Design and Interior Format

Dragonfly DANCE

A MERCY MOUNTAIN NOVELLA

Becca Maxton

Dedication

For Brady

Chapter 1

1977, Ashnee Valley, Colorado

WHAT THE HECK WAS HE doing, saying yes to a blind date? Worse yet, a date his friend Brady set up with some business woman from Boston.

Ben Mannis stood in front of his bedroom mirror, examining the skinny piece of material draped around his neck. Last time he wore a tie was twenty-two years ago when his father and mother passed away. In an instant, he'd become owner of the Mannis ranching empire and ward to his twelve-year-old twin brothers. Chuckling at the ridiculous idea of an empire, he pulled the tie loose again. Ranching was hard work. Harder still was being an older brother, mother, and father to his brothers during their teen years.

He slipped the still-knotted tie over his head, tossed it on the bed, and sat down. At forty-two, he didn't have an inkling if ties were in style any longer. He leaned forward to examine the dress boots he'd shined this morning. Pulling one loose, then the other, he let each drop to the hardwood floor with a thump.

"Why does she need a date as part of a business trip?" Ben asked two days ago while in Brady's office at the local newspaper.

Closing the door so none of his writers at the *Ashnee Valley Gazette* would hear, Brady replied, "It's not really a date. More like showing her around town. Catherine is the publisher's daughter from Boston." Gesturing to the reporters outside his office door window, he continued. "The two of them have no clue. I'm pretty sure she's coming to shut us down. Smaller newspapers are closing, Ben. A lot of publishers are consolidating. It's the Seventies. That's the way of it."

"If you're not losing money, I don't see how cutting off one small newspaper for a town of fifteen thousand is smart business. How much does this operation cost, Brady?"

"We're not in the red, but we're also not making much profit even though our distribution is county-wide. And I agree with you. So for the sake of this town, my writers, and this weekly newspaper, I need to try to prevent her closing us down. *If* that's what she's coming for. Your family goes so far back in Ashnee Valley, I figured you'd be the one to convince her there's something special here."

"Tell me the plan then."

"Well, that's it. You *are* the plan."

Ben stared at his oldest friend. "What?

"I'm told you're easy on the eyes."

Ben lowered his chin. "You're kidding me." He tracked Brady, who started pacing the room.

"The girls in high school used to practically claw each other's eyes out over you. At least they did before you swore off ever being married."

Crossing his arms, Ben widened his stance.

There was no swearing off. I was so busy ranching and raising my brothers, I couldn't date, let alone marry.

"Besides, you own the largest piece of land in this county. You're basically the last-standing founding father of this town," Brady persisted. "You're my best friend and…"

Glancing up, Ben caught the eye of one writer near the office window, watching the two men talk.

"And what?"

Brady shoved his hands in his pockets and faced him. "You're the only bachelor I know. Plus, Catherine is older."

Ben pinched the bridge of his nose as Brady blabbered on. "Not as old as you. I mean, not old, old. She's not a spring chicken. She's single too."

"Are you expecting me to sleep with her?"

Brady barked a laugh and waved his hands. "No, no, no. I mean, yeah, if you want to. Of course not. Especially if you aren't attracted to her. Wait. That came out wrong. No."

"You realize this isn't much of a plan."

"I know."

Ben squeezed the back of his neck. Life did seem a bit mundane lately. "Okay. Sure. "

"Really?" Brady walked from behind his desk.

"I mean, thank you. Seriously?"

Ben shrugged. "I can't promise I can make the case for this town or the newspaper, but if you think my squiring old Catherine around Ashnee Valley for a day helps, then of course I'll do it."

Practically falling into him, Brady enthusiastically shook his hand. "You're a good friend. I owe you."

"Yep. So I'll be seeing you every day at the ranch during calving season."

Ben hid his smile as Brady rolled his shoulders, loosening sore muscles in anticipation.

"Right. Thank you, Ben."

Picking up his boots, Ben returned them to the back of his closet. He grabbed one of the five shirts hanging neatly in a row next to the five pairs of non-work pants. Taking off the dress shirt, he donned his standard weekend outfit. Levi's with a brown belt. Instead of one of his denim shirts, he broke out of his routine and chose a navy and white checked one.

Back in front of the mirror again, he combed his hair with his fingers and put his hat on. When he got downstairs, he took out his tan suede jacket from the hall closet. It was September and still hot, but evenings after the sun went down were cool. Sitting on the bench in the mudroom, he pulled on the cleaner of his two favorite pairs of comfortable boots. Ben slapped his hands to his knees, stood, and opened the door.

"Well, old Catherine, ready or not, here I come."

The plan, if you could call it that, was for Ben to come by the newspaper around eleven o'clock to take Catherine on a tour of Ashnee Valley, ending with supper at Patsy's Diner on the west side of town. Reaching Main Street early, Ben pulled into the Wash 'n Go to get his truck washed before heading to the *Gazette.* He watched the soap smear back and forth on the windshield.

What if she's not used to riding in a pickup truck?

None of these thoughts were ordinarily a concern for him. Or ever. Ben preferred his simple, discreet, and best of all, scheduled, love life. His trips every other Saturday to visit one of the single women in the next town suited him fine. He met his lady friends' needs, they met his. Everyone got what they wanted. No one got more than they bargained for.

Today he'd miss his regular routine of driving the backroad running along the Talking Fish River before heading west and eventually coming around the other side of Mercy Mountain. He'd miss eating a homemade meal, often the highlight of his week. Second only to a satisfying roll in the hay afterward. Ben was an attentive lover, or so he'd been told.

I do all right.

Rolling down his window, he offered the kid drying his car an extra dollar. "Get all the windows and mirrors. I'm looking to impress someone."

"Fancy truck, mister."

"Thank you, son."

With his truck polished, Ben headed off down Main Street. He drove past the post office and the turn off toward the senior center before pulling into a parking spot. It wasn't glamorous, but the *Ashnee Valley Gazette* was headquartered directly above Gordy Sinclair's Hardware Store. He stepped out and waved to Mrs. Gordy through the store window. Officially, she was Mrs. Sinclair. But for as long as he could remember, everyone called her Mrs. Gordy. He guessed she must be eighty years old now. It didn't seem the time to switch things up and start calling her by another name.

He winced at the inordinate amount of noise the creaky wood steps made while he walked up the narrow staircase to the second level. So much for a subtle entry, he mused. At the top of the stairs, he opened the glass door with the stenciled words *The Gazette* on it and stepped into a scene filled with a handful of people singing.

Removing his hat, he stared at his friend Brady playing a banjo at the front of the room. Even Brady's wife, Alicia, their two older boys and five-year-old twin girls were there. A petite blonde woman led the entire room in singing "Take Me Home, Country Roads" by John Denver.

What the heck?

When the song ended, the tiny group clapped enthusiastically. The blonde, who Ben quickly surmised had to be *old* Catherine, was anything but. She was a modern day Grace Kelly with slim, modest curves in all the right places and a face bordering on aristocratic.

Stunning.

Watching her attempt an awkward curtsy for the crowd sent a jolt of electrical thrill up his spine. On the highest heels Ben ever saw, the blonde spun around, tripped, laughed it off, and picked up a tray from the table behind her. She began handing out cupcakes. Mesmerized, he flinched a little when someone touched his shoulder.

"Ben, you've got to meet Catherine," Brady said. "She's the most fantastic woman. Have you ever met a person who knows all the words to every country song ever written?"

"I can't say that I have."

"Catherine," Brady called across the room while pointing at Ben, "this is Ben, the one I told you about."

"You mean my tour guide?" she called back. "He's so handsome, Brady, are you sure that's him?

Brady quivered all over, laughing at Catherine's teasing. This was certainly a side of his friend he'd never been witness to.

Setting down the tray of cupcakes, she put her hands on her hips. "You aren't playing with me now, are you?"

"No, ma'am. This is him!"

Ben enjoyed the form-fitted grey tweed suit Catherine wore as she walked his way. The skirt was long, past her knees. Black buttons ran up the skirt on a slant. The matching jacket was tied tight with a belt around the waist.

A little big city. A little old-fashioned. A whole lot classy.

He stepped forward holding out his hand. "I'm

Ben Mannis, tour guide. At your service."

"Catherine Kendall," she said with a strong handshake. "Kendall Publishing and wanna-be country singer."

He smiled. "What, no cupcake for me?"

A flush crept across her skin and to his chagrin she let go his hand. She crossed the room, picked up a cupcake, and headed back.

Ben chuckled. "I was kidding, darlin'."

What made me drum up that endearment?

"I don't know where my manners went." She handed him a chocolate-frosted cupcake with a wink. "I never kid about treats. Darlin'."

After saying goodbye to Brady and the rest of the newsroom, Ben held the door for Catherine, and they headed downstairs. He'd seen her falter twice on her shoes already and worried she might teeter on the steps, but she managed the descent like a pro.

"My truck is the white one right in front," Ben said, taking the lead and walking around to open the passenger door.

He stood back as Catherine took hold of the safety handle inside the vehicle and made a valiant attempt at lifting her knee against the restraint of her skirt. Failing to get her foot on the runner, she glanced at him.

"Give me a minute. I can do this."

"Of course. There's no hurry."

Her hand on the handle again, she wiggled her behind like a cat ready to pounce then jumped with both feet.

Ben bit the inside of his cheek to school his

expression. "Hold on. I think we need a plan that doesn't involve you falling in the street. How would you feel about me picking you up?"

She wrinkled her nose at him.

Adorable.

"We'll do this quick. No one will be the wiser." He glanced above her head at the two reporters who had their faces mashed against the newsroom window. Brady gave him a salute.

Straightening her skirt, Catherine held her arms out to him like a child. "Okay, you can pick me up."

"Uh, well… I'm going to have to do this more like we're crossing the threshold on the way to the honeymoon suite. I mean as far as the style of lift."

Catherine lowered her sunglasses, looking him right in the eye. "Should I pretend I don't know we have an audience?" Without waiting for his answer, she stepped forward and wrapped her pretty arms around his neck. "Or should we give them something to write about?"

With one arm supporting her back and another under her legs, Ben swooped Catherine off her feet, suggested she duck her head, and placed her on the seat inside the truck.

"I'm pretty sure we just made the front page," Ben said.

"It only matters if we're above the fold. And, thank you by the way."

"My pleasure, old…" He stopped himself just in time. "My pleasure, Catherine."

Chapter 2

CATHERINE PRETENDED TO FUSS WITH her purse in the ten seconds it took Ben to walk around to the driver's side. To her overactive imagination, she still had her arms around his neck when_he'd picked her up and briefly held her. She pulled the sun visor down to look in the mirror, changed her mind, and snapped it back in place. The last way she wanted to appear was vain—or worse, like she was checking herself out.

Getting in the truck, Ben placed his hat between them on the seat then buckled up.

"Ready?"

"Yes." Although she planned to look away, instead she studied the lush hair with a dash of salt and pepper he kept hidden under that hat. With his profile to her, she could see humor lines around his eyes and clean-shaven skin tanned by the sun. She leaned into the outdoorsy scent of pine and soap and man.

How could it be this polite, handsome man is still single?

She might only be a publisher's daughter, but she had the curiosity of a reporter. She wanted the answer to that question.

"Everything okay?" Ben asked.

"What?" She jolted at the sound of his voice. "Yes, just fine. Thank you. Oh wait, shoot." Her gaze darted around the truck. "I left my suitcase upstairs in Brady's office."

"I'll get it. You sit tight, darlin'."

He was gone in a hurry, returning just as quickly to put her suitcase in the truck. After he climbed back in, he put his hands on the wheel and faced her direction.

"I want to apologize to you."

"Whatever for? You've been nothing but polite."

"I'm not sure where it's coming from, but I've called you darlin' twice now. It's not even a word I've ever used before. I'm afraid it may keep slipping out."

"That is curious. It sounds more southern than western." She lifted a shoulder. "I don't mind. I kind of like it."

Especially with your accent and those incredible blue eyes fixed on me.

Picking up his hat she touched the rim. "May I?" When he gave an easy nod, she placed the hat on her head, slanting it low over one eye. "Besides, it's not an apology if you plan to keep doing it. How do I look?"

He leaned back studying her. "You look pretty as a picture, Catherine."

She took the hat off and carefully placed it

between them. "You look pretty as a picture, *darlin'*." She corrected and pressed her lips together when his grin widened.

"Where are you staying? Do you want to stop there first? I can keep myself occupied if you want to settle in before we get going."

"I'm staying at the bed and breakfast on Mulberry. It was that or the motel off the highway. I should check in and drop off my bag. I'll change my shoes, if you don't mind."

"Good idea." Ben backed the vehicle out, made the green light two blocks down, and turned right. They drove past the farmers' market set up under tents in the parking lot of the grocery store. She made note of The Queen B Bookstore so she could check it out later. Not a single art gallery. Not that she would have expected one in a town this size. Maybe it could be a welcome addition. They drove another block past small houses with well-maintained yards, sprinklers, and swing-sets before stopping in front of a charming two story house.

"The Sinclair B&B," Catherine read the sign out loud. "Weren't we just parked a few blocks away at Gordy Sinclair's Hardware Store?"

Unbuckling his seat belt and opening the door Ben answered, "Yep, everyone calls it the Gordy B&B. His daughter runs it now. The Sinclairs, who own it, live next door. You couldn't be surrounded by better folks than them in Ashnee Valley."

She took off her sunglasses to put them in her purse as Ben circled the truck. He opened her door and held out his hand. After a step down on the runner, she jumped with both feet to the ground and stumbled. Ben's hands on her shoulders stopped her forward momentum.

"Clumsy landing." She clutched her purse in a death grip against her chest.

She didn't mind Ben's brief attention as his gaze swept down her body. After all, she was busy taking in his height and broad shoulders. A peculiar expression appeared on his face, to the point she touched his arm. "Is there something wrong? Would you rather not go on this tour, Ben? I know Brady set this up. It's okay if you don't."

"Catherine." The slow-build smile on his face tempted her to reach out and trace the curve of his bottom lip. "There's nothing I'd rather be doing than spending the day with you."

Her heart screeched to a halt, then bit by bit recovered to a rapid flutter.

"I bet you want me out of these ridiculous shoes as much as I do, don't you?" she asked. "Maybe this dressy skirt too."

"Well, that's an interesting thought." He winked and shut the truck door. She shivered when he put his hand on her elbow, gesturing for her to lead the way along the stone path to the porch.

When Catherine entered the B&B, she noticed how cool the room was with the blinds closed against the sun. An enormous vase of flowers sat on the coffee table next to two armchairs in the small lobby. To the left of the door was an antique desk with a fancy stained glass lamp. A kaleidoscope of colorful light formed a halo around the woman sitting behind the desk.

"This is Lucy Sinclair," Ben said gesturing to the attractive older red-head. "She's the owner of the establishment. Lucy, this is Catherine Kendall from Boston."

Coming around the desk, Lucy greeted her with a warm handshake. "Hi, Catherine Kendall from Boston. Pleased to meet you. I'm the one your assistant spoke to on the phone to set up your reservation. I understand you're here to decide if the newspaper sticks around or goes kaput."

Catherine glanced at Ben. "Is that why everyone thinks I'm here? To decide the fate of the newspaper?"

"Aren't you?" Lucy asked when Catherine faced her again.

"Is that what you were told on the phone?"

Catherine turned to Ben again. "Is that what you thought too?"

He nodded.

Oh, she planned to have words with her father. It was just like William Kendall to try to sabotage her. He knew perfectly well her trip was not about the newspaper. He assured her there was no danger for a paper as small as the *Ashnee Valley Gazette*. Still, he had made her promise to pay a visit to the *Gazette* during her trip, and she'd met that obligation already. Embarrassed, she picked up her suitcase.

"I don't know what to say. To either of you. I…"

Ben stepped forward. "It's business. I don't think anyone here likes the idea of it, but even Brady understands the newspaper isn't making a lot of money."

Catherine averted her eyes and inhaled. The idea that everyone in Ashnee Valley thought she was here to rip away their weekly newspaper horrified her. She didn't want to be in the publishing business. She didn't want to live in Boston. This sort of behavior was exactly why she wanted out from under her father's insistent wing. And exactly why she'd agreed to his dare. If she could make a go of her art in two months, she could continue. If she failed, she'd return to the family business and put the idea of being an artist behind her. She tugged the hem of her suit jacket then adjusted her lapel before looking up.

"I'm not here to shut down *The Gazette*. The newspaper was a flimsy excuse for me to make the trip. Part of a deal I made with my father. It doesn't matter. This is awful. I should leave."

Lucy, who had moved closer all the while she spoke, took the suitcase out of her hand. "Leave? Don't be silly."

"What does it matter now? Everyone must think I'm a monster."

Ben offered a bemused smile. "We don't think you're a monster."

"Well, first impressions are important and maybe mine isn't the best."

With a wave and a guffaw Lucy appeared to

dismiss her worries. "Nah, you just got here. Besides, the whole town is more caught up in speculating on whether you and Ben are going to get married someday."

"What?" Catherine put a hand on her hip and pointed at Ben with the other, waving him over. "Do you think you could come over here and stand next to Lucy, please? That way I can face both of you at the same time while I die of embarrassment."

Ben chuckled and crossed the lobby. Lucy moved back behind the desk and slapped a guest book on the counter.

"Here's what you do." Lucy handed Catherine a pen. "Check in. Then go on with Ben to see the sights. Meanwhile, I'll let on that you being here has nothing to do with the newspaper. This gets everyone yapping about why you're really here. Then you go to dinner at Patsy's tonight and you clear it all up." Lucy brushed her hands together. "Easy as that."

Catherine looked at Ben, perplexed. "How does that work exactly?"

"It would take more than an afternoon to explain how fast the rumor mill works in a town this small. Actually, you've already seen it in action. Lucy's right. She'll stoke the fire and when we get to Patsy's tonight, you can share with everyone why you're visiting."

"Everyone?" Her voice rose an octave. "The whole town? But...isn't...aren't my reasons... my business?"

Lucy snorted. "With all due respect, not hardly."

Ben gave Lucy a scolding look. "Catherine, it is your business, but if you want to clear up the newspaper misunderstanding, then you have to give the gossips something."

"Like a speech?" She spun the bracelet on her wrist several times.

Ben wiggled his eyebrows at her. "That is, unless you want to toss out our wedding date."

Catherine laughed despite herself. "I'll go freshen up. What room am I in, Lucy?"

"Up the steps, last door on the left." Lucy's ears turned bright red, competing with her ginger-colored hair. "I put you in the bridal suite."

Catherine picked up her suitcase and headed toward the stairs. "Of course you did."

Chapter 3

Ben took Moon Ridge Road west heading out of town toward a special place he wanted to show Catherine. The Talking Fish River was visible the entire route through the canyon. The water ran high and rapid in some areas.

Glancing at Catherine, he chuckled at the animated way she chewed the spearmint flavored toothpick she'd picked up from the B&B counter after coming back downstairs. She still wore her long skirt with the buttons. Less formal, she'd combined it with a short sleeve black sweater and flat shoes. Her questions about the trees and fly-fishermen dotting the river's edge kept Ben entertained as he drove the winding road.

"Can you imagine waiting for the school bus on a road like this?" Catherine sat forward as they passed a small cluster of homes. "What a life, to grow up where you have all this as your playground." She laughed. "I guess you know what I mean."

Through her eyes, all of Ashnee Valley suddenly seemed brand new. The fresh feeling of her rapt attention expanded his chest, and he joined in, pointing first to a rock formation that looked like a man's profile. He searched for hawks to show her while he kept the truck from crossing the white line. He spotted an eagle and bit his lip to avoid laughing when Catherine stretched her neck to see, bumping the side of her head on the window glass with a thump.

"I would love to sculpt wildlife." She rolled down the window. "That's why I'm here."

"To sculpt?"

"Yes, plus my pottery," Catherine explained. "I have to finish my current sculpture while I'm here."

"Sounds like an interesting hobby."

"See, that's the thing. It's not a pastime." Catherine rolled up the window. "Or at least I don't want it to be. It's what I want to do for the rest of my life. I want my own gallery too."

"So the publishing business isn't your dream?"

"No. Publishing is my father's passion. I'm pretty sure having a daughter who isn't interested in the family news industry is a major disappointment. In fact, he's been searching long and hard for a husband for me. First, so he can have the son he never had, and second, so there is an heir to carry on without him seeming to dismiss his only child's inheritance."

He grumbled at her sentiments despite Catherine putting up her hand to stop him.

"It's okay. I've accepted I am not everything my

father would hope. He's frustrated by this trip to explore my 'hippy inclinations' as he likes to call my art. For the moment, we've struck a temporary truce."

"Is that the deal you mentioned earlier?"

"Sort of. But I'd rather hear about you instead. Is ranching your passion? Have you always known that's what you wanted to do?"

"Yes." He shot a glance at Catherine then back to the road. "The ranch and the boys became my responsibility when my folks passed away. But, now," he nodded, "it's what I know best. It's my passion, as you put it."

Turning the truck off the main street, he crossed a narrow bridge and turned onto a dirt road leading up a hill. He pulled his truck to a stop in a small parking area.

"Would you be okay with climbing the rest of this hill?" he asked, pointing to a path near a rocky area. "I want to show you somewhere special."

"Sure," she said grabbing her bag. "I brought my tennis shoes."

Coming around the truck, he opened the passenger door and waited while she slipped off the flats she wore. "It's sort of a claim to fame around here," he continued. "You can't say you've been to Ashnee Valley without seeing this."

"Sounds exciting, let's go." Catherine jumped out of the vehicle and set off toward the well-worn path starting at the opposite end of the dirt lot. Swinging her arms, she slipped twice on the gravel *en route.*

"Hold up." He jogged a couple steps after her. "The path up ahead flattens out after a rocky area. But for a short distance at the start, it could be a challenge with what you're wearing."

Catherine turned to face him. "Do you want to know what I wear when I sculpt?"

Ben walked ahead of her a few steps on the path and glanced back. "An evening gown? A tiara?"

"Very funny. No. I wear pajama pants, a t-shirt, and a man's dress shirt as a smock."

"What man's shirt?" Ben winced at the jealous note unexpectedly coloring his tone.

Catherine smirked. "How about a piggy-back ride?" She circled her finger at him. "Turn around."

He obliged, turning and bending forward, waiting for her to climb on. She hesitated, her hands on his shoulders. He glanced back and smiled. "Jump on."

"Um, my skirt is too long and tight. I wanted to wear something nice for dinner so I didn't change."

"You should have worn the pajama pants." Ben added, "We can come back another time. I didn't warn you about the climb."

Catherine slapped her hands on her knees, head bent. "Oh, what the hell." She began unbuttoning the black buttons from the bottom of the skirt until only a couple near the top of her thighs were left fastened. When she flapped the two sides of the skirt open and closed Ben caught an enticing view of long, shapely legs. "When we reach the top, I'll button up again."

Ignoring the way she circled her fingers at him, Ben grinned and shook his head. "You're not at all what I expected, Catherine Kendall."

Facing the path, he put his hands behind him and caught her when she jumped on his back. Holding her legs behind her knees he stepped over small rocks and vines on the narrow dirt path that ran between larger boulders. Dipping at one point to hoist Catherine further up his back, he trudged forward.

"Not knowing what to expect keeps things exciting. Don't you think?" Catherine whispered.

Her breath tickled his ear. He turned his head and found them so dangerously lip-to-lip close, he straightened and Catherine slid off his back. He avoided blatantly watching as she re-buttoned her skirt while he caught his breath.

Shoot. Then again, there is the trip back down the hill.

Taking her hand, Ben led her to an area beyond the rocks where the river could be seen far below and pointed. "See it?"

"It looks like a dragonfly. Am I right?" She smiled. "The river looks like the body of a dragonfly and the trees on either side are sort of shaped like dragonfly wings."

Not everyone could see it right away. It pleased him she did. "Yes."

"It's beautiful. Did someone plant the trees that way?"

"That's part of the fun." He winked. "No one knows for sure." When she stifled a yawn, he motioned toward a stand of rocks. "Let's sit for a few minutes and catch our breath. It takes some adjustment to get used to the elevation. I brought some water."

Along the way, he noticed how Catherine stopped to touch every plant. Picking up a simple twig, she twirled it between her fingers.

"I wish I'd brought my sketch pad," Catherine said.

"We can come back again." He tempered his enthusiastic suggestion with a cough.

They sat on a boulder warmed by the sun. The breeze lifted strands of her honey gold hair, sending the fragrance of her shampoo past his nose. She tipped her head back, her brown eyes closed, a flush outlining her high cheekbones. Grateful a bee buzzing in a nearby clover patch was their only companion, he shut his eyes and inhaled a deep breath.

"Ben?"

"Yes?"

"You mentioned you inherited the ranch when your parents died. May I ask when that was?"

"Ah. I didn't finish my story." He opened his eyes again. "My father had a fatal heart attack. It happened far from the house. No one found him until after dark. He was fifty-five. I was twenty."

"That's terrible. I'm so sorry."

"It was a long time ago."

Catherine scooted closer to him. "What did you mean by the boys became your responsibility?"

"I have twin brothers. They were twelve at the time. It was especially hard on them."

Catherine leaned into him, her body a perfect fit against his side. The tender way she traced a finger along one of the veins on the back of his hand resting on his thigh soothed and tantalized.

"And very hard on you too," she said. "What about your mother?"

"Mom was broken-hearted after Dad died. Two months later, she passed away during the night." He drew in a deep breath. "Everyone in town knew. She'd taken some pills. Mixed the wrong medications together by accident. Or maybe on purpose. The result was the same. After that, Ashnee Valley took care of the three of us."

"I don't know what to say."

He turned his hand over, feeling comfortable in an unfamiliar way when she intertwined their fingers.

"Tell me more about this place. The story of Dragonfly Hill. Is that what everyone calls it?"

Her gaze had a softness making it hard to look away. She worried her lower lip between perfect white teeth. He almost lost it when her moist tongue ran the length of that same lip.

"Well, the story is, this is where couples come to declare their love. In my family, my grandfather asked my grandmother to marry him here. My father asked my mother right here on this rock."

Catherine sighed. "That is incredibly romantic."

"Women always love that story." He flinched playfully when she gently pinched his bicep.

"In all this time there hasn't been someone special enough for you to ask for their hand here too?"

He shook his head. "Nope. I missed my chance. Taking care of my brothers and running the ranch took all my energy. By the time I surfaced, everyone was matched up."

She squeezed his hand.

"I'm content. How about you? Do you have someone special in Boston? Maybe someone different than a man your father would pick out?"

When Catherine let go of his hand, he rubbed his palms together at the loss.

"I've secured my reputation back home as difficult to please—at least in the marriage department. My plan is to keep it that way."

He looked up at her when she abruptly stood and smoothed her skirt.

"You know what? I'm hungry. Should we head back to go to Patsy's Diner so I can clear up this newspaper scare everyone's concerned about?"

He rubbed his chin, embarrassed by his confessions and her swift change of topic. On the path down the hill, Catherine took his arm, using him for balance.

"We're a pair, aren't we? A couple of reluctant bloomers."

Chapter 4

BEN PULLED THE TRUCK INTO the parking lot at Patsy's Diner and shut off the engine. With her eyes closed, Catherine took a deep breath and put a trembling hand to her chest.

"I am ridiculously nervous. What if I overshare and make things worse?" She glanced at Ben's profile. So handsome with his strong chin and a mouth she would call very kissable. And patient. Nothing like the busy-body businessmen she'd been subjected to back in Boston. In the last year, she'd suffered through the parade of romantic prospects her father thrust her way. He was determined to marry her off to any lawyer, doctor, professor, or worst idea of all, publishing executive.

"Don't be nervous," Ben said. "Speak from your heart. People here are curious. It's a good chance to engage everyone in your art. Tell them about your plans for your own gallery someday. Did you enjoy seeing the local area today?"

"Very much. It means a lot to me to know

more about you too." Catherine glanced down. "The things you shared with me."

When she caught his gaze, her heart thumped. She picked up her purse and set it on her lap. "I clammed up on you out there at Dragonfly Hill." Her voice was quiet. "I'm sorry." In the confines of the cab, the apology made the air around her feel taut and electrically charged. "There is an attraction between us. Am I right?"

"There is." He rubbed the back of his neck. "We'll have to keep ourselves in control in there." He tilted his head toward the restaurant.

She pressed her lips together adoring his light-hearted teasing. Opening the door, she turned back. "At least through dinner."

The outside of Patsy's Diner was simple with a white cinderblock foundation. The sign above the front door had a pink background with white letters surrounded by red neon lighting. She imagined at night, the sign shone like a beacon beckoning to the hungry. Since the parking lot was packed, it was no surprise the restaurant was noisy and full when they entered. One table remained open. Unattended. Smack in the middle of the room. Her stomach did a flip and drop, settled only by Ben's hand on her lower back.

"Smile. I'm here," he said.

"Thank you, darlin'," she whispered, winning his smirk at her sass.

A hush fell over the dining area when Ben held a chair for her. She nodded at the curious faces. Relief washed over her at seeing Brady Wheeler waving enthusiastically from across the room.

Lucy from the B&B discretely gave her the okay gesture as if to indicate *the plan is working.*

"Hey, Ben." A pretty young woman in a pink uniform with white collar greeted them and provided menus. "Welcome to Patsy's Diner, ma'am, we're very glad to have you."

"I would feel much less nervous if you called me Catherine." A few snickers bubbled up from nearby tables.

"I'd be happy to, if you'll call me Patsy."

"Thank you, Patsy. It smells wonderful in here, like fresh bread and grilled meat all at the same time." Her mouth watered.

When Patsy left, Catherine glanced around the room and spoke to Ben, barely moving her lips. "Off to a good start."

She frowned when he raised his menu in front of his face, only his eyes showing and said, "Get ready."

"You should have the meatloaf, dear," a woman at the table next to them suggested. Ben's eyes slipped out of view.

Is he chuckling behind there?

Turning in her chair, Catherine gave the brightest smile she could. "That sounds perfect."

"Are you going to have the mashed potatoes or the fancy rice pilaf?" the gentleman at the same table asked.

She wasn't sure she could smile wider but she made every effort to. "Would you have a recommendation?"

"No," the man said abruptly. "But there is a right answer and a wrong answer." At that, the man's wife brought a menu swiftly down on top of his head. Shocked, Catherine covered her mouth with her hand. The entire room burst into laughter.

Ben pushed back his chair and stood. Catherine admired the way he took his time, nodding at several people individually before addressing the room.

"Okay, everyone. This is Catherine Kendall. She's from Boston. Her father owns Kendall Publishing. Among many other newspapers across the country, they own the *Ashnee Valley Gazette*. She's going to have a nice dinner and then maybe if we don't scare her off, she'll share a little more about why she's here visiting."

Squeezing her hand into a fist beneath the table, Catherine tilted her head and offered Ben a toothy grimace as he sat back down. He mouthed "what?" when her glare registered.

"How am I, let alone anyone else, supposed to eat when your introduction left everyone on pins and needles about what I might possibly say?"

She put down her menu and scooted back her chair to stand. All eyes on her now, she sucked in a staccato hitched gulp of air.

"I don't know about all of you, but I'm not going to be able to enjoy my meatloaf if we wait." She raised her eyebrows in question at the gentleman at the table beside her. "With the mashed potatoes, by the way." He nodded his approval and she wiped her brow in faux relief. Her new town audience laughed.

"Yes," she began again, "I am the daughter of

William Kendall of Kendall Publishing."

Why am I speaking like the Queen of England?

"I'm from Boston," she barreled on. "I..." She looked around the room, took another huge breath, and unloaded rapid fire, "I'm single. Never married. Thirty-six years old. I still live with my parents."

Several chins dropped.

"Granted, I live in a separate house," she backpedaled. "But it's on the same property."

Raised eyebrows joined the dropped chins.

"I'm not living with my parents, in other words. I'm too old for that."

What the hell am I talking about?

Straightening her shoulders, she continued, "I don't enjoy living in the city. I've always wanted to live near a mountain. I'm an artist."

A few tentative smiles indicated the room might swing in her direction again. "I'm a sculptress. I make pottery too."

Several whispered conversations sprung up at the tables.

"My father isn't fond of this idea. He says it's poppycock." Sympathetic tsk-ing noises made her smile. "I...I just...want to be...where I can do my art. So if you have any questions while I'm here, I'll be happy to answer them." At that, she flounced back into her seat, cringing at the humor in Ben's eyes.

God help me.

Lucy wildly gestured at her from the other side of the room. "Yes, Lucy, you have a question?"

"Um, no. I think you forgot something, Catherine."

"The newspaper," Ben said.

"Oh!" She stood again. "And I'm not here to shut down the *Ashnee Valley Gazette*. In fact, the last thing I want to do is interfere with your town newspaper. Of course, if I can help…" She waved her hands in surrender. "No. Sorry. I take that back. I have two months for my art. That's the one reason I'm here."

She sat, put her napkin on her lap, and with a shaky hand lifted her water glass to her lips.

"So much for not oversharing," Ben teased.

She rolled her eyes. For a brief moment, conversations at tables around the restaurant picked up again. When a hand rose among the crowd in her direct line of sight, Catherine couldn't pretend she didn't see it.

"Yes?" Any talking that had resumed came to a grinding halt. "You have a question, for me?"

Attention turned to an elderly woman in the southeast corner of the restaurant with her hand still in the air.

"I have a question for Ben."

"Yes ma'am, Mrs. Gordy, what is it?" Ben said.

"First, let me say something to Miss Kendall. I know how difficult that must have been for you. Looking at all these strange faces expecting you to pour your heart out to us on your first day here in Ashnee Valley." Embarrassed glances skittered around the room. "I, too, arrived here as an outsider, a very long time ago."

"We love you, Mrs. Gordy," someone shouted.

"That's all well and good," Mrs. Gordy answered,

"now hush. I met Gordon while a student and after graduation I came to visit him. I stayed. This is a wonderful town. I hope you will always feel welcome here, and I will look forward to your art shows."

Tears welled in Catherine's eyes at the kind words. "Thank you." Overwhelmed, she stared down at the table and adjusted her silverware in an attempt to compose herself.

Ben leaned in. "That's about as good an endorsement as you can get."

"Now Ben," Mrs. Gordy said clearing her throat. "My question is this… I believe the room would be interested in hearing from you. What are your intentions? It's high time you quit taking yourself around Mercy Mountain every other weekend to fraternize with the women there. Especially when someone as wonderful as Miss Kendall is here now and directly under your nose."

Chapter 5

BEN APPRECIATED CATHERINE HAVING THE good grace to eat her dinner and leave the restaurant before she laughed at his moment in the spotlight with all of Ashnee Valley watching.

"You enjoyed that, didn't you?" he said as the truck bumped along the dirt road heading back to the B&B.

Catherine gave him a playful look. "I like Mrs. Gordy."

"Do you believe in love at first sight, Catherine? This town does."

"Oh come on, people can see an attraction between us. You're single. I'm single. It's natural for the town to want to push us together." She faced him, putting up her hand as if to take an oath. "I promise not to upend your life."

"What if I want you to?" He fiddled with the radio to find a weather report and also dial back the risk he took saying something so direct. "It's already 8 o'clock. Are you tired?"

"No, not really, why?"

"If you're up for it, I'll show you one place more, up the road toward Mercy Mountain."

"Okay."

Ben made a U-turn on Moon Ridge Road and headed toward the foothills. After twenty minutes, he pulled into the parking area of an old lodge. Reaching across to open the glove compartment, he took out a flashlight. "Hold on, I'll come around for you."

Circling the truck, Ben opened the passenger door and placed his hands on top of the door frame. "You are a very beautiful woman."

Catherine swung her legs toward him and lifted one hand to his arm. "You're not so bad yourself, Ben Mannis." Her touch burned. "If you want to kiss me, this would be a good time to do it."

Keeping his hands on the roof the car, he ducked his head inside the cab and did just that. Softness and a hint of peppermint met his lips, encouraging him to linger and nibble a bit. Her hands slid around his waist, resting a bare second before trailing up his back. He groaned and gave into temptation, hauling her out of the truck and holding her against his chest, in no hurry to finish their first kiss.

She nibbled back for a moment, then edged backward, running a thumb over her lips.

"It gets cold around here once the sun goes down." He removed his jacket and draped it over her shoulders. It was dark enough so only the outline of Mercy Mountain could be seen. "Come on," he said, taking her hand. He turned on the flashlight and used it to guide her around the outside of the lodge to the back deck. Sitting on the steps, he waved Catherine to join him. She settled on the stair in front of him.

"Look up." With his hands on her shoulders he gently pulled her back against his chest.

"Oh, wow. I've never seen so many stars."

"See the Big Dipper?"

She wrapped her arms around herself and he wrapped his arms around her. "I do. It's beautiful here."

"You're beautiful here, Catherine. Why did it take you so long to get here?"

She tilted her head ever so slightly. Unable to resist, Ben placed a gentle kiss on her cheek.

"You know," she said, "I think I do believe in love at first sight. The stars, I mean."

"Very funny," he mumbled in her ear.

"Tell me about this lodge. Why is it not in use? Who owns it? Can we get inside in the daytime?"

He could barely make out the silhouette of her face. By the enthusiasm in her voice, he imagined her smiling. "I could talk to the real estate broker."

"It's for sale?"

"It's on the market.

"I wonder why no one's bought it. I would think it would be snapped up immediately."

"It's been in the Wheeler family for years."

"Brady Wheeler, from the newspaper?"

"Yes, actually his wife Alicia's family. It's hard to tell in the dark, but it needs a lot of work, and for whatever reasons, she has always hesitated. I guess they have decided to just sell."

"Well, I'd love to take a look. It could make a wonderful art studio." The stair creaked as she shifted, her hand brushing dangerously close on his thigh. "Then I think the only other place I haven't seen today is your ranch."

"That's right. Would you like to spend the day with me tomorrow?"

"I'd like that very much."

"I better get you back to the B&B then so you can rest." He ran his hand down her arm. "Ranch life begins early. If you want the full experience, I'll have to pick you up before dawn."

"I'm okay with that."

Ben didn't want to let her go. He'd rather stay here kissing her all night on the deck or better yet, take her back to the ranch so he could make love to her. Turning the flashlight on again, he waited for her to stand, then took her hand and led her down the stairs to the truck.

As they drove toward town, his imagination revisited the gentle kisses they'd shared like sweet torture.

She's way out of your league, pal.

He tapped on the steering wheel, keeping time with the warring voices in his head.

Or you could kiss her again.

Ben swung the truck to the side of the road, put it in park, and faced Catherine.

"What is it?" she asked.

"I'm a grown man. Forty-two years old. I'd like to kiss you like a man who knows what he's doing, not like a school boy who just gave you his letter jacket."

"Oh."

Fuck.

"Right now?" she asked.

Stupid.

Ben closed his eyes. He heard her unclasp her seatbelt and felt the softness of her breast against his arm when she slid over on the seat next to him. Opening his eyes he saw by the dash lights she was shaking her head.

"Ben."

"I can't see your face."

"If you kiss me again, I won't want you to stop. And that might not be a good idea since we're in a truck. Maybe, instead, I could bring an overnight bag with me when I come to the ranch tomorrow."

His heart skipped with a whoop and a holler.

Yes.

"You know Lucy at the B&B can hold a secret for a couple hours in an afternoon, but she won't be able to resist the tongue wagging she can fire up if you don't go back there tomorrow night."

"I bet."

"Don't get me wrong Catherine, I want you. I want you to stay with me. Hell, I want to take you with me right now. But you need to sleep on the idea. You need to be sure."

"It doesn't seem possible that we only met today, does it?"

"Oh, I don't know. I feel like I met you a long time ago and have been waiting all this time for you to come home."

Resting his hand on hers he squeezed when Catherine intertwined their fingers, the same way she had earlier in the day at Dragonfly Hill. Just when he got used to her warm hands in his, she straightened her fingers, removing them from his grasp. By the time she gently patted his hand, as if to say goodbye, he already missed her. He'd best cool it with the romantic talk, he reasoned, when she refastened her seat belt. There was nothing sophisticated enough about a rancher to keep a woman like Catherine's attention for more than a fling.

The phone in the B&B bridal suite rang at 4:30 the next morning. Catherine grabbed the pillow beside her, held it over her head, and groaned. Less than a minute later a knock at the door sounded. She lifted the pillow.

"Yes?"

"Catherine? It's me Lucy. Just making sure you're up. Ben called to say he's on his way."

Sitting up, she swung her legs off the bed. "How much time do I have?"

"About twenty minutes. I'll get the coffee started and see you downstairs."

She acknowledged the offer with a mumble and headed to the bathroom to shower and dress.

Fifteen minutes later she opened the bathroom door allowing the steam to dissipate and put her toiletries into her overnight bag. Before they'd parted the night before, Ben had requested she think about spending that night at the ranch. All night, she had dozed off and on doing exactly that. The two of them were opposites. Opposites attract. Why not have an adventure? This morning she was sure of what she wanted – and who.

After brushing her teeth, she pulled on her jeans, tucked in her white t-shirt and wrapped a yellow cardigan around her shoulders. Arriving at the bottom of the steps, she headed immediately toward Lucy, who held out a thermos.

"You're a life saver, Lucy."

"So you're spending the day on the ranch," Lucy said after a conspicuous glance at the bag Catherine placed on the chair in the lobby.

"That's right."

"Well, I'll look forward to hearing all about it," Lucy paused, "later tonight?"

The headlights from Ben's truck showed through the open blind covering the front window. His arrival gave Catherine an excuse to hurry and to not answer.

Avoiding the wide-eyed look from Lucy, she raised her thermos in thanks and headed out the door.

Ben held the passenger door and reached for the bag.

"Good morning." She stepped up on the runner and took her seat.

"Looks like you thought about a few things last night."

Lifting her chin, she pressed her lips together. "I thought about all kinds of things."

He surprised her, leaning in for a quick kiss. "It sure is a beautiful morning, isn't it, Catherine?"

"It is."

The rising sun gave the foothills a dusty pink hue as they traveled the twenty minutes from town to Ben's ranch. Turning onto the property, they drove under a large wooden archway. To the left were two barns, one big and one small. To the right was pasture with grazing cattle. The land rose to a hill she couldn't see beyond. Straight ahead at the end of the dirt road stood a one-story log house with a nearby corral and horse stable. By comparison to the land surrounding it, the home appeared modest. When Ben pulled into the circle drive and stopped the truck, a handsome young man emerged from the barn nearby and opened her door.

"Welcome to Mannis Ranch, ma'am. My name's Ray Henner."

"Thank you," she said, taking the hand Ray offered to help her down.

"You're welcome, ma'am," he said with a tip of his hat.

Coming around the truck, Ben put a hand on her lower back. "Ray, this is Catherine Kendall. She's our guest for the day."

Ben tossed his keys to Ray. "Make that *my* guest." She bit back a smile at his correction.

Ray chuckled before heading around to pull the truck out of the driveway.

"I don't think he was flirting with me, Ben."

"Trust me. He was. He won't be the last cowboy to do that, either."

A little giddy, she dropped her bag on the ground then tripped forward. "Really?"

Ben caught her by the arm preventing a fall and tapped her playfully on the nose. "I have something inside for you, come on."

The house wasn't as modest as it appeared from the outside, but it also wasn't sprawling. Throughout the house were wide hardwood plank floors and log walls. From the front entry, she could see through to a large living room at the back of the house. Graced with a vaulted ceiling, the warm-hued room had enormous windows that framed Mercy Mountain in the distance. He showed her the kitchen off to the right, which was quaint and cheery with maroon appliances and yellow curtains with tiny red berries in the pattern. They went down a hallway, past a guest bedroom and into the master suite, where Ben set down her bag. From the closet he brought out a large box and set it on the end of the bed. He tipped his head. "This is for you."

Catherine came closer. "You got me a present?"

"More like I'm providing a necessity for a day of ranching."

Lifting the lid, Catherine clapped her hands in delight. "A cowgirl hat!"

"Not exactly. See there are cowboy hats, and then there are rancher's hats."

Catherine pulled the tan hat from the box. "I wish I could say I can tell the difference in hats. It all looks western to me." She glanced around the room looking for a mirror.

Ben pointed. "Try the bathroom."

Standing in front of the mirror, she placed the hat on her head and adjusted it several ways.

"I love it! Am I doing it right?"

When he didn't answer and stepped behind her, she looked at his reflection next to hers and the goofy grins on their faces.

"Ben?"

"Yes."

"Do you believe in love at first sight?"

"I sure do, darlin'. If we don't get going soon, I'm going to stay right here and show you how much."

Catherine took off the hat, fanning her face with it as she followed Ben back outside.

Chapter 6

CATHERINE USED THE BACK OF her hand to cover a yawn as Ben drove back to the house.

"Are you hungry?"

"Ravenous," she answered around another yawn. "Seriously, I could eat a horse."

Ben laughed heartily. "How about I put steaks on the grill?"

"That sounds perfect."

He took his eyes off the road to glance at her. "Yeah?"

"Thank you, Ben. This has been one of the best days of my life."

"Me too." He parked the truck, got out, and walked around to open her door. "Let's go inside." Catherine looked skyward when Ben pointed up. "Looks like rain."

Dark and cool, the house was welcoming after a day of unrelenting sunshine and heat. Within seconds of their entering the house, the first raindrops begin to plink against the windows and roof. He hung his hat on the hook by the door, doing the same with Catherine's when she handed it to him.

Two hats look better there than one.

Sitting on the bench in the mudroom, he took off his boots. Catherine sat next to him to remove her tennis shoes. The white canvas was caked with dried dirt. He placed both pairs on the small rug.

"I hope those weren't a favorite pair of shoes." He began a mental checklist of items to purchase, including boots. The white t-shirt she'd worn all day now had brown smudges. A streak of dirt ran across her forehead. Leaning toward her, Ben gently nudged her with his shoulder. When she turned, he grazed her jaw with his thumb and kissed her once. And once again.

Two kisses tempt better than one.

"Grilling is out. It's pouring." He gestured toward a nearby window. "I hope a simple supper will be okay. First, we both need to take showers. Do you want to go first or should I?"

Suddenly, he became aware this meant Catherine would be naked and in close vicinity. Ben glanced down her body while doing his best to look nonchalant.

"I'll go first." She got up and headed toward the bedroom then stopped and turned back. "Should I use the bathroom in your room?"

He nodded absently.

Two naked bodies feel better than one.

By the time Catherine emerged twenty minutes later, he had come up with an idea for supper.

"Hi," Catherine said entering the kitchen wearing a different pair of jeans and another white t-shirt. Her shampoo or soap gave the kitchen the aroma of fresh cut flowers. Like a bee to a lilac, the scent drew him to where she stood.

"You smell fantastic." He grinned. "I better catch up. How does grilled cheese sandwiches and tomato soup sound?"

"Sounds cozy. It's perfect." Catherine headed toward the living room, calling to him over her shoulder. "I'll watch the storm while you get cleaned up."

In the shower, Ben quickly washed his hair and soaped his body. He shaved in record time, slipped on a fresh pair of jeans and a clean shirt, then headed toward the living room. Finding Catherine asleep on the couch, he quietly continued to the kitchen to make dinner. After he set the kitchen table, ladled the soup, and put the sandwiches out, he returned to the living room. Not wanting to startle her, he sat on the ottoman next to the couch and let his hand skim her hair.

"Dinner's ready."

Opening one eye, she peeked at him. "Did I fall asleep?"

"You did." He smiled. "Ready to eat?"

Sitting up, she swung her legs off the couch and raised her arms overhead in a stretch. Putting out a hand, he led the way to the kitchen, where he pulled out a chair at the table.

"You know what I liked best about today? The way it all seemed so ordinary."

"Ordinary?" he asked between bites of his

sandwich.

"That's the wrong word. Natural. It all seemed natural and comfortable."

"Being outdoors can bring those feelings."

Catherine rested her elbows on the table, her hands beneath her chin. "It wasn't just the outdoors."

Ben added pepper to his soup and stirred. "Why the two month deadline for your art?" he asked, glancing at her. "Is this part of the truce with your father?"

Catherine pulled the cardigan off the back of her chair and put it on. "Yes."

When she looked up from fiddling with the pearl buttons on her sweater, Ben waved his question away. "It was a great day. Anything else is none of my business."

She rested her chin on her hand, studying him again. "I want to tell you." A crease formed between her eyebrows. She ran her finger over it and sat up straight. "It's not a truce. It's an ultimatum. I have two months to finish a sculpture and sell it for at least ten thousand dollars."

"Or what? An ultimatum always includes an 'or what'?"

A knock at the door interrupted their dinner. Ben groaned and excused himself. His steps heavy, he cursed whomever was at the door.

"Ray, what can I do for you? I thought you would have headed home by now."

"Hey Ben, I hate to do this to you. I know you have a guest and all. There's a gate open in the east pasture and several cows have wandered through. The storm is a problem. I don't think I can get them all back onto your property on my own. I'm real sorry."

Ben glanced at the sky outside the door. It wasn't all that late or dark. While the rain had stopped, the air was thick and the sky ominous with an odd green color. He stepped back gesturing for Ray to come indoors.

"Have you had any supper yet?" Both men startled when Catherine leaned around the corner from the kitchen.

"No ma'am, but that's alright, you finish yours." Ray turned as if he was going to head out the door again. "I'll get your horse saddled, Ben."

"Don't be silly, we're practically finished, and it sounds like you should eat something before you and Ben head back out. Am I right?"

Ray gave him a questioning look.

"Better do what the lady says. Go have a bite to eat. I'll get my rain gear on.

Ben stomped off to the bedroom to change his clothes, all the while listening to Catherine and Ray in the kitchen.

Damn it.

He slammed a dresser drawer and looked up to find Catherine leaning against the doorframe with her arms crossed. She entered the room and shut the door.

He unbuttoned his shirt. "Is Ray happy with his food?"

"I don't think you care one lick how Ray is doing at the moment."

"You're right."

He pulled a long sleeve t-shirt over his head and pitched his other shirt into a hamper.

I'm supposed to be in the kitchen getting fussed over, not him. Then I was going to take you to bed.

"Aren't we supposed to wait an hour after a meal before we dive into the deep end of the pool anyway?"

"Very funny. I'll be late."

"I'll be here when you get back."

He slammed his closet door. "We're not done talking about this ultimatum."

Catherine stood in front of him and took both his hands in hers. "I'm going to watch a movie or read a book, and you can wake me when you get back."

"We better get going, boss." Ray's voice boomed outside the door. "The rain is picking up again."

Catherine let go and put a hand over her mouth to hide a laugh when he rolled his eyes. Ben stepped close, placing his hands on her waist. "Will you do something for me? If it gets very late and you're ready to go to sleep, get into my bed, okay? Because, I'm going to think about finding you there the moment I return."

He pulled her in for a hug enjoying her arms around him and the sensual feel of her soft breath as she nodded agreement against his neck. Leaning back, he looked into her pretty brown eyes, capturing the vision in his mind like a photograph he could tuck in his pocket.

Outside the house, Ben gestured for Ray to go first toward the barn.

"How bad is it?"

"There's several cows that went through so I don't think it's minor.

This is going to be a lonely, cold, wet night.

"We'll have to try to herd the cattle back through the gate. Let's hope this lightning doesn't spook the horses. I need the open air to cool down anyway. I mean cool off." Ben stopped walking. "Hell."

Ray laughed. "She is a great-looking woman. I'm sorry I had to interrupt."

"I appreciate you getting me," Ben said, "but keep your eyes to yourself."

Five and a half hours in, the cattle were back through and the gate closed. Ben's thoughts wandered to Catherine and whether she would be worried at the sound of the wind howling. His house had a tendency to creek and moan on a night like this. He lowered his head to stop the rain from pelting his face and closed his eyes. He conjured up an image of Catherine curled up on his couch.

"Hey!"

A hard tap on his shoulder made him sit up, surprised. Ben stared at Ray's grinning face in the pouring rain.

"Whatcha dreaming about?"

He made a point to remember Ray was a good sport and had a work ethic beyond many ranch hands he hired – even if he was being a smart ass at the moment.

"I'm dreaming about sleeping. We done?"

"We're done, boss. I'll meet you back at the house."

"You know, Ray, it's late. You're welcome to stay at the house tonight. It will only be a few hours until we're up again."

Ray leaned close, a steady stream of rain dripping off the brim of his hat. "Thank you, but I'll head home and be back in the morning. Tomorrow is Sunday. Luke and the others will be around. We got the ranch covered. You might consider taking a day off for once."

Ray walked back to his horse and left before Ben could respond.

Back at the house, he said goodnight to Ray who offered to take care of the horses, and headed indoors. Sitting on the bench in the mudroom he removed his muddy boots and rain gear, and left everything in a soggy heap on the floor. Stopping for a drink of water in the kitchen, he absorbed how different the house felt, knowing he wasn't alone tonight. When had he ever experienced a longing like this? It wasn't the anticipation of sex, although he would say that was a good part of his focus. He'd never had a woman spend the night in his home. For years he couldn't with his younger brothers around. He got in the habit of always going to them.

It wasn't like he rushed out after the sex. He liked the feel of a woman in his arms, the pleasure and the afterglow. Never thought of it as more than that. Never considered wanting a woman in his house when the sun rose. Never before this.

Ben put his glass in the dishwasher and returned to the mudroom to hang up his raingear and clean the mud from his boots. Stripping down to his underwear, he threw his dirty clothes in a basket by the washer and walked to the bedroom. The door was slightly ajar and a sliver of light from the bathroom cast a soft glow. He could make out Catherine's shape in the bed. She'd left the blinds open, the windows framing the still-raging storm. He made his way to the shower, then put on a clean pair of boxer shorts and crawled into bed.

Catherine's rhythmic breathing was relaxed and steady. How easy it was to lie beside her. He'd worn his city girl out. To wake her seemed too… raring to go.

It's different now. With her.

He closed his eyes and drifted into a deep sleep.

Chapter 7

BEN WASN'T SO EXHAUSTED HE didn't enjoy the way Catherine ran her hand along his upper arm, then moved on to stroke his hair.

"I like that," he mumbled not opening his eyes.

The sheets rustled as she shifted closer, her front pressing against his back as she continued to run her fingers through his hair. When she kissed his shoulder, he glanced back, then turned over to face her. Hands clasped and held beneath her chin, she appeared innocent enough. Ben changed his mind when she punctuated the look she gave him with a seductive brush of her tongue across her upper lip.

"Hi."

"Hi, yourself. What time is it?" he asked.

"Five a.m. Do you have to get up soon?"

He shook his head. "I'd be late already if this were a regular day." He took one of her hands and began kissing the tips of each finger. "Today is special. I'm taking today off." Ben tucked her hand to his chest, laying it flat against the quickening pace of his heart. "So, I can sleep in."

"I guess I better let you get some rest then." Catherine winked and attempted to roll over.

He put a hand on her back, stopping her progress, and pulled her flush against him. "I'm not that tired. Besides, I want to continue our conversation from last night."

"Right now?" With each breath, her breasts nudged against his chest. "You want to talk? You sure?"

Leaning in, he kissed her, tasting the minty flavor of her mouth. "Did you just brush your teeth?"

She touched a finger to her lip. "I did."

"Hold on." He headed to the bathroom, closed the door, and brushed his teeth. He had a silent conversation with his morning wood to ask if he could please walk back to bed without it poking its head out of his shorts. This proved futile. The shy smirk on Catherine's face confirmed this when he lifted the covers and lay down.

"I'm minty fresh too. Now, what's the rest of the ultimatum?"

Catherine sat up and pulled her nightgown over her head. His eyes slipped to her breasts. All that creamy white skin. A streak of early morning sunlight through the open blinds cast a pattern of lines on the wall behind her.

"Should we close the shades?"

"You're avoiding the question," he answered, resting on his elbow and outlining one rosy tip with his tongue.

"I both finish and sell a sculpture in two

months, or I rejoin the family publishing business and shut up about art."

Ben chuckled. "That's ridiculous."

His hand went straight to her back, supporting as she arched, pushing her breast closer.

"It is ridiculous. But it's always been expected that I would take over the family business someday. I'm a grown woman trapped by my father's whim."

Ben pressed his lips together, giving the gentlest pinch to her nipple. When she moaned, he let go to look up at her face. Eyes closed, head back, her hands behind her on the bed.

"Sounds like you have nothing to lose," he said, dipping a little to look her right in the eye when she whipped her head forward.

"I have everything to lose is more like it. This is my one chance."

"What if we set you up in the small barn? There's plenty of space. You won't have to worry about meals or traveling to and from the B&B to somewhere. You can get started right away. You can work all night, every night if you want."

He cupped her other breast and plucked the raised peak with his finger then lowered his head and fluttered his tongue around the tiny nub.

"Mmm, let's come back to this conversation later."

Ben noticed a new deepness to her voice and shifted toward the middle of the bed. He put his hands on Catherine's waist. Instinctively, she lifted her leg to straddle him. Now, he had equal access to both beautiful breasts. Taking his sweet time, he visited one globe then the other like a honeybee floating between flowers in summertime. Catherine squirmed against him. He imagined all her senses on fire for him. He wanted her to be so desperate she'd shatter the moment he entered. The ache between his legs pulsed. He pulled her head down to meet his lips, coaxing her tongue in a dance with his. As their kissing grew more passionate, his hands dropped to her bottom to smooth and squeeze. Catherine hissed when he pressed directly against her core. Breaking the kiss, her lips parted, eyes shut, his name escaped on her sigh.

"Tell me what you like." He dragged her up and down his body. "What feels good?"

Catherine raised herself higher, hovering over him. He closed his eyes as she took over the intimate rhythm. Up and back.

At the sound of her soft giggle, he opened his eyes to find her smiling down at him.

"I knew it'd be like this," she said.

Her intoxicating movements held no hesitation. The sheer lack of timidity in her statement planted their lovemaking on equal ground.

Ben eagerly flipped her onto her back, answering her confidence with his own. He reveled in her small squeal of delight as her arms wrapped around his neck. He gave over to his appetite, touching his lips to every inch of skin as he trailed a path of kisses down her neck.

"You smell good, honey."

She pulled the pillow from under her head, accidentally sideswiping his cheek with it when she tossed it off the bed.

"Oops. Oh…" she moaned the words as he drew her nipple in his mouth again. Suckling hard, he grazed lightly with his teeth.

"Oh my God, yes."

"You like that?"

"Harder," she answered.

He ventured lower, his lips traveling down her stomach. Lifting his head he looked his fill at the soft blonde curls at the apex of her core. So inviting. So pretty. He separated the folds with his thumbs and blew a wisp of cool breath as Catherine lifted her hips.

Swirling his tongue, he drew the tiny bundle of nerves into his mouth. On Catherine's whispered "please" he slipped one finger, then two into her warmth. The first wave of her orgasm fluttered when he curled his fingers.

One of many. I hope.

The moment struck so sweet, he smiled then pressed his tongue flat until her climax was spent. When she slipped her hand into his hair and gently tugged, he lifted his head.

Her gaze was misleadingly lazy when he stood next to the bed to kick off his boxers. Like a tigress, she stalked his every move with eager eyes. He pulled a condom from the bedside table and pushed the blankets off the end of the bed. Languidly, she raised her arms above her head, her cheeks flushed by desire. She was every bit a goddess.

He groaned her name, utterly unnerved when she grasped her hands to a bar on the bed frame and locked her eyes with his.

"You're so beautiful. So perfect." He took a deep breath, knowing his simple words were inadequate. But her shuddered breath told him differently and hurled him into a longing so deep he wanted to possess everything about her.

Proud.

Humbled.

He lowered himself, settling into the cradle of her hips, womb and soul joining them together. Between kisses, Ben tried to catch his breath. She met every thrust of his with her own, answering his arousal with matching energy. A groan escaped deep in his chest at the exquisite clasp of Catherine's muscles tightening the silky channel surrounding him. He wasn't going to last much longer. Bracing himself on one arm, he tenderly traced a circle with his thumb as the faintest hint of Catherine's climax stroked him. On her moans, he sped up, savoring every sexy twitch and shiver coming from beneath him.

"Don't stop. Don't stop. Ben!"

His hips bucked, rocking, until he followed in his own release.

Amidst the scent of sex hanging in the air and soft fingers sliding across his back, Ben slowly descended to earth.

"I'll be right back," he said against Catherine's lips.

On weak legs, he left her for only a moment to dispose of the condom. On his way back to bed, he pulled the sheet off the floor and draped it over Catherine. He lay down and wrapped his arms around her.

"So," he said after a long minute, "you said you knew it would be that way?" Her body shook against his side with laughter. "Damn, woman." He kissed her forehead and pulled her close. "Because I had no idea. No idea it would be like going from love at first sight, to died and gone to heaven."

Catherine opened her eyes, surprised by the time. Sitting up, she stretched her arms above her head, then headed to the bathroom. After slipping on the robe she'd left hanging on a hook, she emerged to find Ben awake and waiting. He patted the empty space next to him.

"Take all that off, honey, and come back here."

She put her knee on the edge of the bed, then lay down on top of the covers, her head resting on his chest.

"That sounds like a good plan. But first, I'm starving. I want to make us breakfast." She smiled. Ben caressed her scalp, his fingers running through her hair.

"This morning was incredible, sweetheart."

She nodded against his chest. "It was."

"And now, you want to make me breakfast? Pretty sure if you feed this stray cat, you'll have to put up with me forever."

She gulped in a breath and clung to him, her arm tightening around his middle. Her cheeks heated, caught off guard by a single tear falling. Dipping her chin, she nodded, but didn't speak.

"Hey, now." Ben moved his hand up and down her back. "What just happened? All the air went out of the room. Did I say something wrong?"

She shook her head, her cheek still nuzzled against his chest. Another tear escaped.

"Look at me, honey."

She sat up, letting him see her face, and brushed the back of her hand to her wet cheek.

"Come here, Catherine."

He opened his arms and she tucked herself into the crux of his shoulder. His chin rested on her head.

"We're more than I imagined," Ben said. "Did you feel it too?"

She snuggled closer. "It's terrifying."

At his chuckle, she lightly swatted his chest.

He turned her face to him with a warm strong hand. "It's like waiting for something you can't understand but knowing every second leading up to it was worth it."

With his intense gaze settled on her, her heart threatened to beat out of her chest.

"French toast or eggs?" She blurted the words.

"I want it all."

She sat up, hands shaking as she pulled the lapel of her robe closed.

He grinned, lifting up on his elbows. "French toast *and* eggs *and* you sculpting in my barn."

Covering her face with both hands, Catherine peeked between her fingers. "I don't know. I am a complete mess."

He took her hands away from her face, pausing to kiss the back of each. "What you are is sexy,

Catherine. Let's eat and then you have a choice to make."

"You're giving me an ultimatum too?"

Ben chuckled. "No, honey. It's an offer to help."

"What do you get out of this deal?"

He tucked a wisp of blonde hair behind her ear.

To have a little taste of something I thought I missed.

"I get to witness your dream become truth."

Chapter 8

IT WAS ONE WEEK SINCE she accepted Ben's offer. They'd agreed she'd keep her reservation at the B&B, nonetheless. It was a lame attempt at keeping the town gossip from spiraling into a frenzy. Ridiculous, since she spent every day sculpting in Ben's barn and every night in Ben's bed. All week the rain continued to pour in Ashnee Valley. Thank goodness the storm had finally moved through this morning.

Like any prior day, it wasn't hard for Catherine to find her way around Ben's kitchen as far as equipment needed to make a meal. He had one of every item. One frying pan, one mixing bowl, one spatula. Double checking the cupboards, she sighed in relief. There were enough clean plates and forks so she wouldn't need to take dirty dishes out of the dishwasher to hand wash them.

Definitely a bachelor.

The sound of Ben's shower ran in the background. She set to work, humming and shaking her tail feathers as she enthusiastically whisked ingredients in a bowl. She had just put French toast in the oven to keep warm when there was a knock at the door. Out the kitchen window, she saw a green truck parked in the driveway. Catherine headed to the front of the house, surprised she hadn't noticed the truck arrive. Patting her hair in place, she bit her lip as she opened the door.

I wonder if I look perfectly debauched.

The young man standing on the porch whipped off his hat and his face turned beet red. "Ma'am."

"Hello." Catherine pulled the lapel of her robe together and smiled. "Can I help you?"

"I'm sorry to disturb you this morning. I work with Ben. I mean, I work for Ben, for Mr. Mannis. My name is Luke. Is he here? I have to speak with him."

Catherine kept a straight face at the barrage of words spilling from the man's mouth. "There's nothing to be sorry for." She stepped back. "Please come in. I'll get Ben, make that, Mr. Mannis, for you." She gestured toward the kitchen. "Help yourself to coffee, if you like."

Walking into the bedroom, Catherine went to the bathroom door and knocked.

"Ben, one of your men is here to see you."

Steam escaped when he opened the door. Her gaze dropped from the shaving cream on his chin to the towel around his waist and slowly returned to his eyes.

"Did you answer the door like that?"

She glanced down her body. "Like what?"

Ben leaned forward and kissed her. "Like drop

dead gorgeous, that's what." He dabbed shaving cream from the corner of her lip. "Who'd you say is at the door?"

"Um." Catherine tucked her hair behind her ears for a moment, lost in the haze of hot air and steamy kisses. "A man."

He rolled his eyes and growled. "I swear Catherine, if it's Ray again, thinking this is funny…"

"No," she said, her wits finally returning. "He said his name is Luke."

Grabbing a towel, Ben wiped his face. She backed up so he could pull on jeans and a shirt then followed him down the hall. The young man still stood in the entryway, where she'd left him. He ran his fingers around the rim of the hat he held in front of him.

"What's going on?" Ben put his hand on Luke's upper arm. "Everything all right? You look white as a ghost. Come here, kid. Sit down before you fall down." Ben practically picked up Luke as he pulled him toward the kitchen and plunked him into a chair. "What's happened? Where's Ray?"

"He's in town. At the hospital. He sent me to tell you."

Catherine stilled, barely breathing as Ben pulled out a kitchen chair and sat across from Luke.

"Spit it out, son. Tell me what?"

Luke visibly swallowed and looked down at his lap. "The storm. It…there was flooding last night. Bad. Mainly along Moon Ridge Road."

"Go on," Ben said.

When the young man glanced in her direction, Catherine nodded encouragement she had no business being confident in.

"The road gave out, in a big way, washed away right at the part where it dips down along the Talking Fish River. And there was a car. Brady's car."

Luke's knee bounced.

"Brady Wheeler? From the newspaper?" She moved closer, standing behind Ben's chair, and put her hand on his shoulder.

"Yes. I guess the Wheelers were trying to get back home, up the mountain and out of danger, and the car went over the edge into the river."

Ben's head dropped forward. "Tell me all of it. Were there any survivors?"

"Yes, Brady and his wife and the boys are okay."

"Thank God," Catherine said.

"What about the twins?" Ben raised his head. "Are they hurt?"

Lips trembling, Luke ran his hands up and down his thighs. "Cindy barely survived. Cammie didn't make it."

"Oh no." Catherine held both hands to her chest. "Oh, no. No. One of Brady's little girls? One of the twins? But we just saw them."

"Ray sent me to tell you." Luke stood abruptly. "He sent me. I'm real sorry."

Ben rose from his chair, put an arm around Luke, and walked him to the front door. "I appreciate you being the one to come tell me. You can go on home now."

"I'd rather stay today. To work."

"I understand. And I appreciate it. Thank you."

After saying goodbye, Ben closed the door and

leaned against it. She went to him, burying her head in chest as his strong arms circled her.

"I'm so sorry, so sorry. My heart aches." Leaning her head back she saw a tear spill down Ben's cheek. "I know he's your dear friend."

"I have to get to the hospital," he said and cleared his throat. "You can stay here or you can come with me or…"

"You can drop me off at the B&B. I'll hurry and pack my things." Letting go, she walked toward the bedroom.

"Catherine."

She turned back.

"What we have between us it…matters. Maybe in the face of something like this, this tragedy, it matters even more. To me. You know that, right?"

"Oh Ben. You and I… it has mattered."

"Has? That sounds like the past."

"It matters so much. Maybe more than you will ever know. Because it changed me. But don't you see, my heart…what I want…it's not all possible."

I shouldn't be thinking about myself.

She put a hand to her lips. "Ben, this isn't what's important right now. You need to get to the hospital."

And I need to step up and take Brady's place temporarily at the newspaper. As always, my art will come second to what Dad expects.

Ben dropped Catherine at the B&B in silence, a contradiction to the questions battering around inside his head.

It's not possible? What does that even mean?

He swung his truck into the closest parking spot and walked into Ashnee Valley Hospital. Picturing Cammie, a sweet, vibrant, five-year-old girl gone, chewed up and spit out his heart. He stopped short. Twenty feet ahead of him the Wheeler family stood huddled in a tight circle, hugging one another and crying. The lump choking his throat was the only thing that kept him from letting out a sob. Brady saw him and broke away from the group, walking his direction.

"Don't." Ben waved him to go back. "Don't let go of your family." He took off his hat and hung his head as his friend's arms came around him.

"God damn it, Brady, I'm supposed to be the one comforting you, not the other way around."

Brady's arms fell to his sides. "It doesn't matter at a time like this."

"I don't know what to say."

He didn't see Alicia Wheeler approach.

"Hi, Ben."

Facing his best friend was hard. Facing Cammie's mother wounded him so unbearably, he couldn't speak. He took her into his arms, only releasing his hold eventually to wipe the tears from his eyes.

"I don't know how to do this," Ben confessed. "I'll do anything you need. I'd trade my life if I could."

"I think we all would if we could." Brady put his arm around his wife. "None of us know what we're doing. Cammie was…is…pure love and joy. That's what we have to hold onto right now."

Catherine showered at the B&B with a bittersweet sense of washing off the budding artist to resume her unwanted business persona. She had immediately placed Lucy on communication duty the second Ben dropped her off, asking her to put out a call for a meeting with the newspaper's writers. All two of them. At noon.

Now walking the couple blocks to the offices of the *Ashnee Valley Gazette,* she wore sunglasses, hiding from the inappropriate sunshine on this somber day.

Who do I think I am, scheduling a meeting?

Her father had called her immediately. The flood was national news.

"You are representing Kendall Publishing, Catherine. That's priority."

Oh right. That's who.

For all she knew, she might be the only one to show up at this meeting. She reached the hardware store by eleven-thirty. Gordy Sinclair had offered to meet her there to unlock the office to the *Gazette.* At the top of the steps, she lifted her chin, took a deep breath, and walked through the door.

"Brady! Why are you here?" She covered her mouth with her hand. "Oh, my God. That was an awful thing for me to say." Bowing her head, she took a step back. "I didn't mean to interrupt. I'll go downstairs."

"Catherine. Stay. I'm just picking up my keys. Besides, I know why you're here."

"You do?"

"I'm a newspaper man, remember. Stay. I want your help."

"I'm so very sorry about Cammie. I'm so sorry for Alicia and the children."

He opened his hands in front of him, a gesture of shock and why.

"I'd say it's unbearable, but there aren't words. Nothing will ever be the same. Ever."

She held her breath as Brady paused.

"This didn't just happen near the bridge on Moon Ridge Road. There was flooding all along the river. Four Bears was hit and towns further north. I'm aware of nine other deaths. Cammie…"

"It's so terrible." Catherine moved closer as Brady choked on his words.

"…makes ten."

"I'll do anything you need."

"Funny, those are the exact words Ben said to me at the hospital." Brady touched her shoulder. "He's a good man, you know."

"Whatever you have in mind, I'd like you to go ahead," he said. "This is a small paper, but the freelancers are good writers. I'll need to take a temporary leave. I'd hand over the reins to Bill Brissell as editor, if I were you. He's top notch and ready for it. Nonetheless, this story is way bigger than Ashnee Valley, and they'll need someone with your experience to guide coverage. I expect national news is descending on us as we speak, but I want this town to see the *Gazette* out front. I don't want us bullied out of the way."

"I agree."

He straightened his shoulders and spoke with such passion, she couldn't help but admire his strength. "We write human stories. We write in-depth stories, not the twenty-second sound bites you see on TV. I know you didn't come to here for any of this. That you came for other reasons. To do other things."

Catherine shook her head to stop him. "I know how to do this."

"Thank you. I have to know the stories of the people who died in this terrible flood will be told…I have to know Cammie's life will be honored."

Unable to hold back her tears, Catherine hugged Brady. "I will. We all will. We'll find a way. I promise."

Chapter 9

THE WHEELERS CHOSE THE SMALL chapel attached to the senior center instead of one of the much larger churches on the edge of town for Cammie's funeral. Catherine sat outdoors as long as possible, listening to the leaves rustling and the chapel bell ringing. She watched people in town arrive. A few news reporters from outside Ashnee Valley who hoped to interview Brady or his wife also showed up. She was relieved when Bill Brissell in his new editor role stepped in and cleverly offered the first of the victim's stories. A scoop, Catherine supposed. How she hated the news business. Nonetheless, tomorrow she would start mapping out assignments for the *Gazette*. They planned a feature on each of the ten victims of the flood. She hadn't decided who would write the story about Cammie.

When she entered, Ben made eye contact with her from the front of the chapel where he sat waiting for his turn to read. She gave him a smile, knowing his nerves got the better of him the day before when they worked on the reading together. It wasn't stage fright she realized, it was his desire to get the reading just right. Broken-hearted, he'd wondered out loud if any of this mattered. Cammie was gone. People leave one way or another, he noted. She'd suggested the best way to honor everyone's grief would be for him to read a psalm familiar to most. Walking to the front of the chapel, Ben read Psalm 23. She closed her eyes and listened.

At the gathering after the funeral, Ben introduced her to several more people in town. Not a single person failed to offer to share stories about Ashnee Valley or Cammie if they had known the little girl well. She tugged on Ben's hand. "I'm going to go outside and sit by the water for a few minutes."

"I'll come with you, if you don't mind."

"I would love that."

Catherine sat on a log close to the Talking Fish River rather than the bench at the top of the hill. The tall grasses where water rushed over them lay flat and broken tree branches lined the shore.

"It's hard to believe this is the same river that has caused so much sadness. The water is so calm and peaceful. How did it get the name Talking Fish River?" Settling next to her, Ben removed his hat. "You did a nice job with the reading, by the way. It was beautiful." Catherine reached over and took his hand.

"Thank you. So, let's see, the Talking Fish River got its name long ago, of course. I was convinced my grandfather, Benjamin Mannis Sr., named it."

Catherine's jaw dropped. "Wait a minute, Benjamin Sr. was your grandfather so Benjamin Jr. was your Dad? Does that make you Benjamin the third?"

Groaning, Ben gave her an embarrassed look that made her chuckle.

"Yes. But there are more. My younger brothers live in South Dakota. Fourth and Fifth. And no, if I'd ever had a son, he wouldn't be named Benjamin. Five Bens are enough. That was going to be your next question, am I right?"

"Maybe. Remember, I'm a one and only child."

"You know what I think?" he asked.

"What?"

"I think maybe we'll have time for finding out more about each other. Now that you're going to fill in at the *Gazette* to give Brady some help, things must be on hold with your Dad, right? That means you can stay more than two months." Squeezing her hand, Ben smiled. "After that, there are all the sculptures you want to do, so that's another...I don't know...lifetime?"

Oh, Ben.

Ultimatum or circumstances, it wouldn't matter. In her father's mind, she'd still lost.

"You really are sweet on me, aren't you?" she said.

"I'm too old to be sweet, but yes, I am sweet on you."

"Right back at you. I'm thirty-seven and I'm not sweet either."

"I thought you were thirty-six?"

"About that." Catherine rolled her eyes. "Sometimes my age slips out wrong."

"Do you ever get it wrong going in the other direction?"

She laughed. "You mean like, 'I'm forty years old. Oh, wait a minute! I'm only thirty-five years old!'"

When Ben looked past her without laughing, she turned and found herself facing Alicia Wheeler, who stood a few feet away.

"Don't stop on my account. On a day like today, laughter sounds like music." Alicia stepped forward. "Ben, I was wondering if I could speak to Catherine for a moment."

Getting up, Ben put his hat on and brushed any dirt off his back side. "Of course." He touched Alicia's arm as he passed by.

Catherine gestured to the nearby bench. "Let's sit there, it will be more comfortable." When they settled she asked, "How are you holding up?"

Inhaling, Alicia gave her a look Catherine couldn't interpret.

"It's a physical ache to be perfectly honest."

She put her hand on Alicia's arm. "I can't imagine. How can I help?"

"I'm going to speak about business, Catherine. I don't have the energy to say this another way."

"I'm listening."

She waited as Alicia twisted a tissue in her hands.

"I understand you showed some interest in renting the lodge off Moon Ridge Road for an art studio. I'd like to know if you would consider buying it from me instead."

"Uh…"

"Brady didn't want me to put you in this position. You don't know me or really anyone in this town very well. I realize this might seem presumptuous or strange."

"No, it's not strange," Catherine stammered. "Well, maybe a little. You're correct that I don't know you or others well. I'm getting to know Ben."

Looking down at her hands again, Alicia paused then raised her teary eyes. "My heart. It died. With Cammie."

"Oh, please don't say that."

Alicia raised her hand in pause. "It did. And there's no getting around that and there's no bouncing back. There is only going forward."

Catherine leaned closer. "Maybe you could wait to make any decisions. About the lodge or otherwise."

Alicia shook her head. "The lodge sits on ten acres. Our house is on the same property, you just can't see it from the lodge. I inherited all of it."

"Can I ask why you want to sell the lodge?"

"Because I've never wanted it. All the lodge represents to me is the time my father spent building it, all the while ignoring his children and his wife and spending every last dime we had. When he died, he owed money. Between Brady and me, we've spent a small fortune on it. That money could have been college funds for my kids. Instead, we had to shutter the place and absorb my father's debt."

"Alicia, forgive me for this question, but are

you and Brady in financial trouble?"

Alicia's jaw tightened. "We are. I'm not going to pretend otherwise. I've wanted to put the lodge up for sale for a long time. If you're interested, I could meet you there on Friday and you could see the inside and where the property lines are. I'd let you see our house too, but we haven't yet told the children."

Catherine met Alicia's determined look with wide open eyes. "You're selling your house too? Are you leaving Ashnee Valley?" She instinctively turned, seeking out Ben who watched from a distance. Having no way to answer his questioning gesture, she quickly looked back.

Alicia took one of her hands. "I think if circumstances were different, you and I would become good friends, Catherine."

"If you stay, we could be friends. I'd love that."

Alicia's grip tightened. "We're leaving. Brady accepted a position at a newspaper in Salt Lake City. He's telling Ben right now."

Catherine held her breath and looked as Brady now spoke to Ben. Her heart dropped as the news landed on his face.

Late in the afternoon, after folks headed home, Ben stacked chairs inside the senior center. Catherine pulled the paper tablecloths off each table, crumpling and tossing them into the large trash can. Catching the corner at the wrong angle, Ben forced the chairs to align, clattering the metal legs together violently.

"You don't need to do that," the center director said as she walked toward Ben. "We're going to be setting up for dinner soon. You're welcome to join us, if you'd like."

Grumbling, Ben unstacked a chair, slamming it to the floor. Catherine stepped into his line of sight and tilted her head twice toward the double doors at the back of the room. A nurse wheeled in one of the residents.

She put her hand on his arm and answered the invitation on both their behalf.

"Thank you, but we're going to head out now. This is such a lovely room, with the windows facing the river and the trees. You and your staff made this difficult day more bearable."

"It was our pleasure. Oh, and would you return this photo of Cammie to the Wheelers? It was left on the welcome table in the lobby."

Outside, Ben followed her in silence as she made her way across the parking lot to the truck. He started the engine and turned out of the church onto the road heading back to the ranch.

"We're going the wrong direction for the B&B."

Ben swung the truck around in a U-turn without saying a word. In silence, they passed the fire station and the Queen Bee Bookstore she kept meaning to visit. When they pulled up to the B&B and he cut the engine but didn't turn his head, she studied his profile. His jaw flexed like a ticking time bomb.

"Ben?"

"What?"

"It's six o'clock, how about we call it a day."

"No. What I want is for you to go get whatever you need to stay at the ranch tonight."

"I'll take a pass," she said, declining what sounded like an order. When he simply nodded and restarted his truck, she got out, slammed the door, gave a salute through the window and marched away.

"Catherine."

The truck door slammed and a moment later Ben's hand was on her elbow. "Hold on, what was that? Don't walk away."

Tilting her head she answered, "You seem in a hurry to get back to the ranch. I didn't want to stop you."

"As a matter of fact, I am in a hurry." He ran his thumb back and forth under his chin.

"It's been a difficult day. Let's call it a night, Ben."

"You know, ranching doesn't stop because there's a flood. Or a death. Or because friends I've known my whole life are moving. Or because you want to pretend you would ever stay in a little town like Ashnee Valley."

She sucked in her breath and silently counted to five. "Then don't let me keep you."

"I've been waiting for hours to be alone with you."

She put her hands on her hips. "Is that what this is about? Everyone at the funeral and me, we all inconvenienced you today?"

"You know, you walked away from me on the day Cammie died. You dropped a bomb about how everything and nothing has changed. Now you just stormed away again a minute ago."

She took a step closer, wishing she were taller so she could be nose to nose. "Stormed away? Don't you think that's an exaggeration?"

"Come back to the ranch with me."

"After that performance? Why?"

"God damn it. Because maybe you're not the only one that wants things to be different."

"So you thought it would all be easier if you pushed me away too? I'm not following your logic."

He gently pulled her forward. Her heart sped up at the softness of his lips and the way he slid his fingers into her hair as he kissed her. Even ticked off at him, his touch still made her wiggle her toes.

"I don't know what I'm doing" he said after pulling away.

"Clearly." She softened her remark with a hand on his cheek. "When I said earlier that I've changed and nothing changes, I meant…" She looked down for a moment, kicking a pebble off the sidewalk. "I meant nothing changes because I have to step in, to help manage the *Gazette*. Whether it is my job or a relationship, it will always be that my dreams come second." She closed her eyes, lifting her chin to allow the evening sun to warm her cheeks. "That sounds so selfish."

"You're not selfish, Catherine. You're ready for the life you want to finally begin. Please come home with me."

She pulled his arm and stood on her toes to kiss him on the cheek. "On one condition. While I'm inside for a moment, you work on the angry thing. I get that today's been rough. Brady and Alicia's announcement…well, it stinks. But I'm not coming out the ranch so you can take it out on me."

"I'm sorry."

"I'm here right now. Don't take that for granted."

"I won't."

Chapter 10

HER WORDS WERE THE ASS-KICKING he needed. With Catherine inside the B&B, Ben got into his truck again, put his head back, and closed his eyes.

I need to rein myself in. This was never going to be forever.

After Catherine returned to the truck, they drove in comfortable silence to the ranch. He had more opportunity to calm down when Catherine asked to use his phone to make a few calls.

Heading to the kitchen, Ben pulled a glass out of the cupboard and two beers from the refrigerator. Walking by Catherine in the living room, he gestured toward the sliding glass door at the back of the house leading to the patio.

"Come join me, when you're off the phone."

He raised the large canopy umbrella and angled it to block the last burst of sunlight before sitting down in one of the lawn chairs. He put a beer on the table next to him for Catherine and opened his, taking a long pull. In his right hand he moved the bottle cap from finger to finger, back and forth. Staring at Mercy Mountain, he tried to imagine the Wheeler household. Ben pictured a scene where Alicia and Brady would tell the other children about leaving Ashnee Valley.

Poor kids, everything familiar is being torn away.

When the sliding door opened and closed behind him, he sat up, grateful he hadn't spilled the beer he held against his chest.

"Were you sleeping?" Catherine asked, sitting in the chair next to him.

"Just resting my eyes," he answered. "You were on the phone for a while. Everything okay?"

He waited as she poured her beer in a glass, took a swallow, and set it on the table. Lifting her hair off her neck, she stretched out in the chair, leaned her head back, and turned toward him.

"My father is in the hospital. I was speaking with my mother on the phone. I hope you don't mind, I gave your phone number to her in case she needs to reach me again."

Ben put his hand on hers. "What happened? Is it bad?"

"He's stable. They think he had a small stroke. Apparently, he acted more ornery than usual yesterday. Although that would be a hard thing to decipher. Then his left leg gave out and he fell."

"I'm sorry. Do you need to go back to Boston?"

"Oh no. My father made sure I knew that wasn't necessary." Catherine sat forward on the edge of her seat with her hands clasped. "In fact, he got on the phone to give me a reminder."

"I get the feeling it's a reminder you didn't need or want."

She picked up her beer again. "It doesn't matter."

He didn't like the fatalistic tone of her voice or the way she guzzled her beer. Most of all he didn't like the cave forming in the center of his chest.

"Now I have even less time." She stood, waving her hands dismissively as she paced. "That was the reminder. Sculpt. Find a buyer for it. Oh, and run the newspaper."

"And run the newspaper? Catherine, your father…" He sucked in a breath. "Okay, let's slow down and think about this. Running the paper is not part of the ultimatum. Not technically, right? So, don't do it."

"I promised Brady."

He got up and walked to her. "Hear me out. Wouldn't it make more sense for Bill Brissell to run the paper, anyway?" Ben rubbed her arms as he spoke. "We can talk to Brady together. He'll understand."

She crinkled her nose in the adorable way that made him crazy to kiss her.

"Really?"

"Yes, really." He kissed her forehead, then headed toward the house when the phone rang.

"Well, that was short-lived," Catherine said returning to the patio after answering the phone call from home. "Kendall Publishing is in the midst of a possible takeover by a competitor." She shook her head. "I'd almost think it was another ploy from my father if it wasn't my mother who told me. Everything you said before, Ben, it was a wonderful idea. I wish… I have to go home. I called the airline. My flight is at ten tomorrow morning. It's over two hours to the airport, so I'll arrange a car. I called Lucy at the B&B and she's going to pack up the few things I left in the room and ship them to me in Boston."

Ben couldn't take his eyes off her when she sat down again. "Doesn't sound like you're planning on coming back."

"It's hard to say when. In fact, I better make a few more phone calls. Bill Brissell will have no choice now but to run the *Gazette*. I'll talk to Bill first so I can reassure Brady. And I have to cancel a meeting with Alicia for Friday. She was going to show me the lodge. I'll need to work in the barn all night. Is it okay if I make arrangements later for what to do with the sculpture? Someday it needs to be bronzed. Who knows when I'll ever be able to get that done?"

She certainly had her list of to-dos well in order.

His list had one item.

Goodbye.

He grabbed his beer off the table. "There's no hurry about the barn. I'll give you privacy so you can work tonight. I'm going to take a shower."

Ben left Catherine on the patio, walked to the kitchen, and slammed the bottle on the counter. In his room he left a trail of dirty socks, shirt, belt, and pants on the floor. He stood in his underwear in the bathroom, turned on the shower faucet, and cursed his compulsive tidiness. He went back through his room, picking up dirty clothes along the way, then put them in the hamper and hung his belt in the closet.

Stepping into the shower, he closed his eyes, letting the water soak his body.

Catherine opened the shower door. "Hey," she said, wrapping her arms around him from behind. Her naked body pressed against him.

"Hey." He shifted to face her. "I'm taking you to the airport tomorrow. You're not leaving here in a taxi."

She nodded and leaned forward, kissing his chest, sliding her hand up his thigh to stroke him intimately. Groaning, he shifted positions so Catherine was under the warm water. Gently he washed her hair and soaped and rinsed her body. Lifting her chin with his finger, he kissed her and opened the shower door.

"I don't want to talk anymore about you leaving."

Wet and dripping, he wrapped a towel around Catherine first and another around his waist and led her through the house to the living room. Next to the couch he pulled the knot of her towel loose and then his own, letting both fall to the floor.

"No shyness, Catherine," he said when she blushed. "Let me show you how much I want you."

Laying his towel on the couch, he sat, wanting her to ride and rock him. Catherine put both knees on the couch straddling his lap. When he guided himself to her core, he pushed up as she lowered until all of her soft, wet warmth surrounded him. With her hands on his shoulders and his on her hips, he memorized every bounce and sway of her breasts. Every moan and hitched breath he cherished as her body moved in perfect sync with his, united toward completion.

The more hours that went by after they made love, the more awkward the night became.

Her mother called again to say please hurry. In the wee hours of the morning, he wrapped his arms around her when she finally returned from the barn and fell asleep. Repeatedly, he shoved the idea from his mind that this was the last time she might ever be beside him. Just once, he wanted to experience what it would be like to say the words…

"I love you," he whispered.

Chapter 11

AT DAWN, BEN WENT OUTSIDE to take care of several chores before he drove Catherine to the airport. He caught her watching him from the kitchen window as he returned to the house. He bowed his head, averting his eyes beneath the brim of his hat.

Coward.

Inside, he joined her in the kitchen, saying yes when she offered to fill his thermos with coffee for the ride. When it was time to go, he carried her bag to the truck and opened the passenger door for her.

Hours later, with barely any words spoken between them, Ben pulled up to the departure area at the airport.

"I'll call when I get there," Catherine said.

"Don't forget."

"I won't. I promise. I want to thank you, Ben."

"No." He shook his head. "Don't go there. Go home. Take care of your father. Take care of work." He looked directly at her, mustering a smile when she teared up. "It's okay, Catherine. We don't have time for discussions now."

"You don't think I'll come back, do you? You don't think I feel the way you do."

He got out of the truck without answering and tucked his keys in his pocket. Coming around to open her door, he silently willed her to just leave.

"Is it because I didn't say I love you back?"

She'd heard.

He stepped back, distancing himself. From the question. From his pain. From her.

"Ben, I didn't say it because..."

He took another second step back, one hand up, his eyes on the ground.

Look at her.

He raised his head, glancing quickly away again at the unshed tears shimmering in her eyes.

"You didn't say it, Catherine." He shrugged and gripped the back of his neck. The pain on her face bore into his heart. Busying himself he picked up her bag and dug his keys out of his pocket. "What we had was nice."

"Nice?" Catherine smacked her hands on his chest and pushed. "Don't you do that, Ben Mannis. Don't you dare act that way toward me. I know what you said." She ripped the bag out of his hand. "Don't you dare try to sweep me under the rug. You're just as scared as me."

"Catherine. Go."

"Please don't take your words back."

"I won't. Call me tonight. I'll be waiting." He turned away, got back in the truck, and headed home.

Three weeks after Catherine left, Ben met Brady at Patsy's Diner for a last meal together. The Wheeler family would depart in the morning and head to their new life in Utah.

"Everything ready to go?" Ben asked, taking a seat in the booth across from his best friend.

"The moving truck has come and gone. The kids are sleeping on air mattresses tonight and we set off early tomorrow."

"How's Alicia doing?"

"Okay. Happy to be leaving Ashnee Valley. That sounds harsh, but this town, including the lodge, which we're still trying to sell by the way, holds too much pain for all of us. We still haven't found the right buyer. So I'll be back from time to time until we can unload it. I know Catherine was interested, but now with her father's health and having to leave…"

Ben absorbed the awkward way Brady's voice fell off.

"Where did you and Catherine leave things, if you don't mind my asking?"

Patsy arrived with menus and water, giving him a short reprieve where he could gather up an answer. He thought about the phone calls with Catherine over the last few weeks. There were only three of them. One to say she'd arrived home. The others to update him on her father's health. Hoping for the best, but preparing for the worst, she was occupied with assisting her mother and stepping in at Kendall Publishing. Clearing his throat, Ben kept his eyes on the menu as if he had a lot to consider.

Who am I fooling? I always get whatever the special is.

"I think it is safe to say William Kendall won't be able to keep up the business operations of Kendall Publishing. As Catherine is the only child, I can't see her doing anything other than staying in Boston to keep everything going. It's what has always been expected of her."

He met Brady's look of surprise with an off-handed shrug.

"I'm real sorry to hear that, buddy. She was a breath of fresh air. I sure liked her a lot."

"Me too, Brady. Me too."

After dinner, Ben stood outside in the early November air while Brady circled around every topic they could possibly reminisce about. All of it to avoid saying goodbye.

"Sure, I can come visit Utah," Ben finally agreed. He knew in his heart this was unlikely to happen with his ranch responsibilities. "Let me know whenever you'll be coming back in town."

"I will miss this place," Brady said. Ben's gaze followed his friend's toward Mercy Mountain in the distance. "It's not easy knowing I won't see you around, so I'm going to say a quick goodbye."

Ben swallowed the lump in his throat. "You've always been a great friend. We've had some good times. Give Alicia and the kids a hug for me." The sting behind his eyes forced him to look down for a second. "Drive safe. Why don't you give me a call when you get there? Let me know you've arrived."

"Will do."

With a last half-hearted smile, Ben shook Brady's hand. His arms fell heavy at his sides as he walked back to his truck. The door creaked when he shut it. He started the engine, exhaled, and let go of one more thing he loved, and drove home.

A week before Thanksgiving, Catherine called to let Ben know her father after weeks in the hospital had finally taken a turn for the better. The family was feeling hopeful for a full recovery.

"That's wonderful news. How is your mother holding up?"

"Fierce as always. She's taking on each day like a champ. I miss you."

He put a hand to his chest to still the ache brought on by seeing her smile so vibrantly in his mind's eye. Every morning he opened the shampoo bottle Catherine left behind to enjoy her scent. The hat he'd given her still hung on the hook next to his. At the end of each day this meant something, didn't it?

"There are a lot of details to help Mother with right now. The newspaper business never quits. Ben? Are you still there?"

Hearing his name, he surfaced from the deep. He understood, he told her, making sure to keep his tone light. Their calls ended with promises to talk again in another couple days.

Damn it. This isn't healthy. Eventually one of us will stop calling. Or one of us will stop answering.

Two weeks later Ben, out of pity he supposed, found himself invited for a Thanksgiving meal with the Sinclairs at the Gordy B&B. Not quick enough to come up with an excuse at the time, he accepted and now drove to the festivities with a mood that matched the streets of Ashnee Valley. Cold and deserted.

On a wave of nostalgia, he turned onto Moon Ridge Road instead of heading directly to the Sinclairs'. Snow blew sideways, swirling across the road as he wound the truck through the canyon toward the lodge. Now that the road was fully repaired after the flood, he tried imagining a time when he'd resume his routine of visiting the next town over again. Why should he feel guilty about the idea? There was nothing wrong with thinking about women he used to spend time with before.

"Lonely is lonely," he announced to the air in the truck. His voice buzzed angry and gruff in his ears. Swinging the truck around the bend, his headlights landed on the For Sale sign at the bottom of the lodge driveway. He jerked the truck to a stop. A shiny new addition in large red letters hit him like a punch in the gut.

SOLD.

"Hey, Ben, good to see you. Happy Thanksgiving." Lucy Sinclair opened the door wide and gestured for him to come in. "Can I take your jacket?"

"Thank you. How many guests are you planning for dinner?" This seemed the polite thing for him to ask.

"Just you, me, and my Mom and Pop. We don't have any guests at the B&B right now. Sometimes we do for the holidays. That can be fun, with new people."

Caught off-guard, he stilled, one arm in, one arm out of his jacket. Lucy held tight to the end of his sleeve and tugged it with a grin.

"Chin up, Ben. It will be mostly painful, but bearable. It was Mom's idea. No use sitting out at the ranch all alone on Thanksgiving, she said."

I can think of a lot more useful things, like a bottle of whiskey and football on TV.

"Hell."

"Quite possibly." Lucy winked.

It was during dessert he made the decision to share the ultimatum Catherine had been hogtied to during her brief time in Ashnee Valley. Confessing the details of William Kendall's time limit and demand on Catherine to give up her art drained the last of his energy for the day.

"That's a real shame," Gordy responded.

"I had hoped to see her work," Mrs. Gordy added. "We could use some culture in this town. That seems an unreasonable demand by her father."

"Did she finish her sculpture?" Lucy asked. "What is it?"

Ben glanced up from his pumpkin pie. "She finished it in clay. It has to be bronzed. I don't know what it is."

"You don't even know what she was working on?"

"I haven't been in the barn since she went back to Boston," he mumbled.

Lucy plopped a scoop of whipped cream on her piece of pie. "Catherine left weeks ago, Ben. Did you ask her if it needs to be preserved or whatever one does with a sculpture? What if it breaks or something? It can't just sit out there in your barn all winter."

He left the Sinclairs' thirty minutes later with enough leftovers and embarrassment to last the weekend.

Why didn't I know what she was sculpting? I never even asked. Sure, I offered the use of the barn and put some plywood down as a floor. All I cared about was keeping her close to me as long as I could.

The next morning, Ben opened the door and peeked inside the small barn she'd been using, for some reason acting as if Catherine might be in there sculpting and he shouldn't interrupt.

I know better.

Flipping on the light, he closed the door and stood staring at the sculpture in the center of the room.

Covered by a tarp it was bigger than he expected, although he wasn't exactly sure why he had any impression of it at all. Dinner at the Sinclairs' seemed to burst the bubble he'd created that of being respectful of Catherine as an artist by not interfering with what she was working on. He considered how his lack of interest may have appeared to her as another sign that her art, and therefore she, came second.

It was cold in the barn, but not freezing. He glanced over at the unplugged space heater on top of a workbench, wondering if there was some sort of temperature he should maintain in the barn. He took off his hat, scratched his forehead, and walked forward until he stood next to the covered piece.

"Let's see what we got here," he said to the emptiness as he carefully lifted and rolled back the tarp. It was a figure of a little girl. He could make that out easily because she wore a dress and a ribbon in her hair. "Damn." Ben said softly as he studied the figure from the back. Catherine had captured movement with her sculpture. It was as if a breeze blew through the room right now. The way the ruffles of the skirt showed motion. The way the little girl's hair lifted away from her neck. She was life-size he guessed, about three and a half feet tall.

He pushed the tarp further away from the edge of the sculpture with his foot. The girl's arm reached toward the sky. A dragonfly settled on the tip of her finger. As he moved toward the front, he wondered if this was a sculpture of Catherine herself. Wouldn't that be something?

Ben froze, then squatted before the figure.

Cammie.

The sculpture was the spitting image of Brady and Alicia's daughter. He shut his eyes as images flashed. His father on a gurney being loaded into the ambulance. His brothers' heads bowed at Mom's funeral. Saying goodbye to Catherine at the airport.

He sat on the floor and looked up at Cammie's joyful face.

A couple of reluctant bloomers, Catherine had called the two of them the first day they met. Was she right?

After a long while, Ben stood and gently hovered his hand above Cammie's head. "I'd still trade my life for yours if I could. I wish you were here, for your mom and dad and sister and brothers."

He picked up the tarp and hesitated, as if covering the sculpture would extinguish the warmth of a lantern. With one knee raised, Cammie seemed to be skipping, as if to try to catch that dragonfly at her fingertip.

"I wish you were in the sunshine on Dragonfly Hill so everyone could see your delight."

Chapter 12

CATHERINE TURNED ON THE RADIO in the living room and embraced the cheery holiday music for ten seconds, before flipping it off again.

"You can leave it on," her mother said from her seat on the couch. "It's festive while I watch you decorating the Christmas tree. Would you get that?" she added when the phone rang.

Setting down a box of ornaments, Catherine made her way to the phone in the hallway.

"Hello."

"Hi, Catherine, it's Alicia."

"It's so good to hear from you. How are you and Brady? And the kids? How's Utah? Sorry! Here I am blasting you with questions when you're the one that called me."

"It's okay. We're all doing as well as can be expected, seeing as this will be our first Christmas without Cammie.

"That must be so hard."

"It is. But the reason I'm calling is to let you

know that we're heading to Ashnee Valley right after Christmas. That's why I wanted to talk to you."

"Oh?"

"How is your father doing?"

"He's much better, thanks for asking. We're expecting a full recovery."

"That's wonderful news. So I'm calling because the sale of the lodge fell through. Anyway, it's available if you're still interested. If you want it, you could sign the papers when you come back to Ashnee Valley for the town council meeting after Christmas."

Catherine looked down at the floor. "I have to be in England over the holidays. My father is acquiring a newspaper in London, and I'll be there representing him. What town council meeting?"

Alicia laughed. "It's only the town council meeting about your sculpture. Brady and I are so honored you chose Cammie as your subject. It will be emotional, but we also can't wait to see it. You'll be there, right? Your parents made reservations at the Gordy B&B for it already, so I just figured…."

"Whoa, whoa, whoa. My parents? Hold on a moment." Catherine set the phone down and walked back to the living room.

"Mom, you're going to Colorado after Christmas?"

"Yes, dear."

Catherine held up a finger, then walked back to the phone.

"Alicia, can I call you back?"

Catherine sat down on the ottoman across from her mother. "What is going on?"

"Your father and I were invited to come to Ashnee Valley to attend some sort of event about the dedication of your sculpture."

"Invited by who? My sculpture isn't finished. How can it be dedicated? Dad is going?"

"Oh, he's going all right," her mother said and pointed. "The invitation is over there on the piano. I thought you'd seen it."

As Catherine headed across the room, her mother continued. "In a moment of weakness while in the hospital, your father told me about the ultimatum he had you trapped under during your visit to Colorado. We don't do ultimatums in this house. He either goes or it will be a long cold winter."

"Mother," she said with a burst of laughter. "You do know that's an ultimatum." She picked up the announcement and examined it.

Special Meeting
Ashnee Valley Town Council
December 27 at 7:00pm
At the Sinclair B&B (basement)

Topic:
Dedication of Catherine Kendall's sculpture
Proposal for permanent installment
Public comments welcome before the vote
Light refreshments will be served

"Catherine, you made something that a whole

town wants to talk about. I'll be damned if I'm going to miss it. I suggest you call your cousin Rodney and see if he'll go to England in your place. Oh, and don't forget to call your friend back too."

Catherine crossed the room, hugged her mother, and hurried to the phone.

"I'm coming. To the meeting. I'm interested in the lodge," she said, whispering the last part to Alicia.

"I couldn't hear you, what?"

"I want to buy the lodge. I just…" Catherine cupped the receiver and whispered a bit more loudly, "Don't tell Ben."

"Why would you not tell Ben you're buying the lodge?"

She switched the receiver from one sweaty hand to the other and sat down on a chair in the hallway as Alicia continued speaking.

"Catherine, none of us knows how long we will get to be on this earth. I know this better than most."

"Of course," she acquiesced politely only to be confronted again.

"If you see a chance for your art, you take it."

"It's not just about buying the lodge or sculpting," Catherine stammered. "It's that and so much more."

"All the more reason."

"This is Ben's doing, right? This dedication? It is, isn't it? We left things so unclear."

"Girl, get back to Colorado so that man can ask you to marry him!"

"Well, what if *I'm* the one that's supposed to ask *him* to marry *me*?" Catherine blurted, her heart beating wildly. "Did you ever think of that?" She held her breath. "Oh my God."

"That's the spirit." Alicia snorted a laugh. "What if, indeed."

It was the week before Christmas and snow had started to accumulate. December looked like a holiday card. Ben welcomed the dormancy winter represented for the ranch and his heart. He understood seasons. Spring would eventually come…and summer…then fall…and his heart would mend. At least this is what he tried to convince himself of each night as he lay in bed.

On Sunday morning his phone rang and he picked it up, figuring it might be Catherine, who knew this was a day off for him and he'd be home.

"Hey, Ben, it's Brady. How are you doing? Got any snow there yet?"

He stood in the kitchen, looking out the window at the ranch. The field from this direction looked as if it were covered in powdered sugar, something he and Brady joked about since they were kids.

"Powdered donuts," he answered and chuckled when Brady laughed with him. "How's Utah treating you?"

"Can't complain. The job is busy and we're doing some work on the house we bought, so that keeps Alicia occupied. The kids have school. We need that busyness right now, you know?"

"I imagine," Ben agreed. "It was a beautiful article Bill Brissell wrote about Cammie for the *Gazette*."

"Thank you. But Bill didn't write the article. Catherine did."

He pulled his chin back. "She did? Huh. I didn't know that. She never mentioned it to me."

"She and Alicia have had a lot of conversations, so she could really capture Cammie for us both in the article and her sculpture. I think they've become very close as a result. Good friends."

"There seems a lot I don't know. I didn't realize you knew her sculpture was of Cammie."

"She asked for our permission, and we can't wait to be there after Christmas so we can see it. Hold on a second, Ben. Alicia wants to ask you something."

"Ben?"

"Hi, Alicia, how are you, honey?"

"I'm doing okay. I'm sure you're aware that we sold the lodge?"

His heart thumped hard, reliving the blow when he'd driven by and seen the sign on Thanksgiving night. "Yes, I saw that. I saw the sold sign several weeks back."

"That deal fell through. I couldn't sell to someone I know planned to tear everything down and destroy the land up there. Fortunately, we found a new buyer."

Ben couldn't care less who wanted to own the lodge now. "How can I help you out?"

"Well, Lucy called me and said there are so many people expected for the town council meeting that she wants to move it from the basement at the B&B to the lodge. Are you okay with doing that?"

"Sure, I guess, if you're okay with it."

"It's fine with us. In fact, that way the new owner can sign all the papers while we're in town too. But here's the thing. The owner wants to have everyone stay for a party after the meeting concludes. Sort of a meet and greet, I guess."

Running his fingers through his hair, he forced himself to smile in an attempt to get the tone of his voice to cooperate by matching. "Of course," he answered.

"Great! Consider it a plan."

Not ten minutes went by before Ben's phone rang again. He hung his head for a second, then walked to the kitchen.

"Hello?"

"Ben, its Lucy."

Seeing as Lucy had never called him before, he immediately asked about her mom and dad, all the while chastising a competing thought in his head.

Please don't invite me to Christmas at the Gordy B&B.

"Mom and Dad are doing fine. I was just calling to make sure Alicia had been able to reach you."

"She did," he answered slowly.

"About the lodge for the town council meeting? And the party after?"

"Uh huh."

"Okay, then. Good! I just wanted to be sure. You have a nice day now," Lucy said and hung up.

He put the phone down and walked to the living room. His gaze traveled up Mercy Mountain to the spot he imagined the lodge to be, hidden behind snow-covered trees. Once the New Year arrived, he would let things go with Catherine. It was the right thing to do. Knowing he'd feel the loss of a greater possibility for the rest of his days.

Chapter 13

TWO DAYS AFTER CHRISTMAS, CATHERINE arrived in Colorado. She didn't tell anyone in Ashnee Valley she was coming, until her surprise visit to the Gordy B&B before the sun rose. Keeping Lucy close by was critical to maintaining secrecy. Plus, Lucy was the one person in town who could mobilize help last minute to accomplish her plans.

Finally, Catherine could begin decorating the great room at Mercy Mountain Lodge. Sweaty and covered in dust and dirt, she'd spent all day moving pieces of wood and other construction materials to the edges of the room. She'd swept, and swept, and swept. When the Wheelers closed up the lodge years ago, they clearly hadn't bothered to step foot inside it again. She shuddered at the two dead mice she'd found as she cleaned.

"How's that look?" Gordy Sinclair asked, stepping off a ladder and brushing his hands together. At eighty-something years old, he was the last person Catherine wanted to see teetering precariously up in the air, hanging lights on a tree.

"Don't even try talking him out of it," Lucy had told her earlier before turning to her father. "I'll hold the ladder, Dad."

Exhausted, Catherine dragged one of the many boxes of ornaments across the room and opened it. She had one hour before she'd have to head back to Lucy's to take a shower. She needed to get back before the meeting started and before Ben arrived. Her stomach hit the floor. Did she really have the guts to ask him to marry her? She opened the box, grabbed a tray, and headed up the ladder.

What if he says no? He's not going to say no. Okay. But…what if he does?

"The cavalry has arrived." Lucy pointed to the doorway. Ray, Luke, and several other men who Catherine assumed were from Ben's ranch came inside.

"Miss Kendall." Ray tipped his hat. "I hear there is a tree that needs trimming. Fast. Am I right?"

Smiling, she stepped back down the ladder. "Did you arrange this?" she asked Lucy, who beamed at her with a nod. "Bless you, Lucy."

"We can take it from here," Ray said. "You go on and get ready and we'll have it done and be cleared out before everyone arrives. If we run into any snags, our supervisor will keep us on track." He pointed at Mrs. Gordy, who was busy setting up a folding chair across the room.

At six-thirty, Ben turned off Moon Ridge

Road heading up the drive to the lodge.

This was right. Bringing Catherine's sculpture to the lodge. Bringing together the town to discuss a place of honor for Cammie's memory. Bringing himself to closure of a love he never thought he'd have experienced even for this short a time. Melancholy sat perched on his shoulders and he shrugged it off. He backed the truck to the front door and got out. When Ray or Brady arrived he'd ask them to help move the sculpture.

Heading inside, he flipped on the lights and examined the chairs set up classroom style. A folding table was placed at the front and he walked there, setting down a stack of papers. He'd brought a handout from the artists who did the bronze work on Catherine's sculpture.

Walking to the windows that faced the western side of the lodge, he looked outside at snowflakes the size of quarters falling steadily.

"It's pretty, isn't it?"

Ben turned to find Lucy entering the lodge. She brushed snow off her shoulders and flung her coat on a table at the back of the room.

"See all these chairs?" she asked as she stomped her boots on the mat. "There are a lot of people coming to this meeting tonight."

Ben nodded. "I thought Brady and Alicia might arrive first. I'll need some help moving the sculpture indoors." He glanced outside again as light from another car's headlights tracked across the snowy deck.

"Ray and Luke were right behind me. They can help. Brady and Alicia had a couple guests they were bringing, so they were all still at the B&B finishing their dinner when I left. They left the kids in Utah with Brady's sister. If everything goes right tonight with the vote, they'll all come back in the spring to see the sculpture in place. I bet it's weird for the Wheelers to come back to their old town and have to stay at the B&B." Lucy put another stack of papers on the table at the front of the room.

"I brought some information about the bronzing process. What did you bring?" Ben asked.

"The newspaper article about Cammie just in case there's someone who didn't see it. Although I can't imagine that."

Ben picked up the newspaper and studied the photograph of Cammie, wondering if he was doing the right thing. Maybe this should have been done in private. He wasn't trying to put the Wheelers' grief on display again or relive the day of her death by creating a dramatic moment.

He looked down when Lucy squeezed his arm. "Everyone is going to love your idea, Ben." She smiled. "And the sculpture! I can't wait to see it. The fact that it was bronzed in Four Bears is so cool. Who knew artists of that caliber are right in the town next door? It's a wonderful gift from Catherine and you. Thanks for letting us share this."

It had never struck him as his to share. Any of it. "It's all Catherine. I just…"

"Ben. Ben. Ben." Lucy shook her head as she spoke.

"What?" He followed her up the aisle between

chairs just as Ray and Luke opened the doors.

"Catherine came here to experience life as an artist. You are the one who loved her for being the woman she most wanted to be. That's heady stuff, my friend. That's what women want."

"So, that's what they want? To be or not to be," Ray quipped as he slapped his ball cap against his thigh, shaking off snow.

Lucy laughed. "You're a goof, Ray. Hurry and help Ben bring the sculpture inside. It's almost time for folks to start showing up."

Purposely, Ben kept himself busy, greeting people from town and taking their coats as they arrived. It was comfortable and kept his nerves in check to know everyone's names and ask simple questions about how farms were doing or stores in town or kids at school. Catherine had left them all, including him, with an incredible gift. He was going to see this through, even if she wasn't there.

By five minutes to seven, the room was packed. Four chairs in front were left for Brady and Alicia and the guests Lucy had mentioned. When the door opened he returned Brady's wave as he entered with Alicia and an older couple. He couldn't see a resemblance that pointed him to which side of the Wheeler tree the visiting family must be from.

Ben gave Brady a hug, but missed his chance for other introductions when Mrs. Gordy tapped the front table and called the town council meeting to order. It was seven p.m. on the dot, after all.

"Welcome, everyone," Mrs. Gordy said. "I hope all of you are having a wonderful holiday, and I want to thank you for coming out on a snowy night for this special town meeting. We'll keep it brief. In fact, let's dive right in. We have a party to enjoy afterward, don't we?" Putting a hand out she said, "Ben, why don't you go ahead and explain to everyone why we're here."

The crowd clapped as Mrs. Gordy sat down and Ben slid his chair back and stood. He put his shaky hands in his pockets and cleared his throat.

"Thank you Mrs. Gordy and Lucy for setting everything up. I want to especially thank Brady and Alicia Wheeler for coming all the way from Utah."

"Ashnee Valley will always be home," Brady chimed in. Another round of applause burst from the crowd.

Ben took in the sea of familiar faces along with a deep breath. "Ashnee Valley is our home and earlier this year we lost Cammie, one of our own. There were nine other souls lost in the flood up and down the Talking Fish River. It's been hard to understand…" Ben glanced at several heads nodding in the audience. "Hard to bear," he said, making eye contact with Alicia and Brady. "But sometimes, there is an act of kindness. An act of honoring someone we've lost that doesn't make up for the grief, but it brings comfort. A gratefulness for the time you shared loving them." He gestured to the tarp-covered figure to the right of where he stood. "And I think that's, in some way, the very reason Catherine Kendall came here and why she left us with her sculpture."

He rubbed the back of his neck and smiled.

"Now, I'm not an artist. But I know Catherine intended the sculpture to be bronzed, so that's how I had it finished." Signaling Brady forward, he and his friend lifted the tarp to reveal Cammie's likeness to the crowd.

"Good lord," Brady said and turned to his wife. "Alicia, come close."

Ben stepped away as Cammie's parents studied Catherine's artwork. He glanced at Mrs. Gordy, who lifted her chin and blew out a breath, determined as he to keep a dry eye.

When Brady and Alicia took their seats, Mrs. Gordy stood to address the group again.

"The purpose of this gathering is to bring forth Ben's proposal to dedicate this sculpture of Cammie in the spring for permanent installation on Dragonfly Hill."

Brady's smile beamed his direction and Ben let out a breath for the first time that evening as applause took over the room.

"I'm not hearing any objections, so let's vote, shall we? All in favor say Aye," Mrs. Gordy shouted.

A resounding "Aye" filled the room.

You did it, Catherine.

Ben looked down at the papers on the table in front of him with a smile. "I have some information here about the artists who did the bronze work and an article about Cammie, which Catherine wrote, by the way."

"I'd like to say something," said the older gentleman who had been sitting next to Brady and now stood. "My name is William Kendall and this is my wife, Marjorie. We're Catherine…the sculptor's parents."

Ben straightened his shoulders.

It's wrong you're here and she's not.

Marjorie Kendall turned in her chair to face the rows behind her. "We were so very pleased to be invited by the Wheelers. We're honored to be here. Thank you."

Ben made direct eye contact with Catherine's father. "It's a shame Catherine isn't here and you are."

Lucy's laugh rang out. Closing his eyes, he rubbed his forehead as his words replayed in his head.

"It's a shame Catherine couldn't be here, I meant to say."

"Who says I'm not?"

The air shifted and the hair on his arms stood up as he turned. "Catherine."

"Hi, Ben."

"You're here."

"I am." She walked out from behind the Christmas tree at the back of the great room.

For a second, he couldn't move then suddenly lurched forward. "You were behind the tree the whole time?"

She teetered on six inch heels before him, decked out in a red form-fitted holiday suit with a long skirt and flared jacket held with a thin gold belt.

"You look beautiful."

He raised his eyes to the ceiling at the foot stomping and hoots starting up behind him. Recovering, he held out his hand.

"Come here, honey. Let everyone see the artist."

Chapter 14

PRESSING HER LIPS TOGETHER, CATHERINE joined Ben at the front of the room where he announced her arrival.

"Would you please say a few words about your work?" Mrs. Gordy asked.

"Um, okay," Catherine said as the crowd clapped and then quieted. Her peripheral vision tunneled toward darkness, and she swayed before putting her hands forward on the table in front of her. Ben sat next to her father, staring at her.

Don't faint. Breathe. Breathing is good.

"So, I...when I sculpt it's like breathing. It's like an exhale for my heart." She straightened and put her hand to her chest. "It's about a feeling, an expression of happiness or joy or sadness." Catherine moved next to the sculpture of Cammie, running her fingers along the little girl's hair. "Or all of these emotions. But there's something I didn't really know until tonight." Walking to the front row, Catherine took Alicia's hand. "I didn't know that I could share something this way." She glanced at Ben. "It looks *so* good bronzed." She laughed at her self-praise along with the crowd. "I wanted to honor Cammie's spirit and Ashnee Valley's resilience. It means the world to me the way all of you are receiving it. I guess that's the inhale because my heart is so full. It's overflowing."

Catherine leaned forward to receive Alicia's embrace and landed clumsily on her knees.

I guess that solves however I was going to get down on one knee in this skirt.

She remained on her knees and scooted two inches at a time to the left and hugged Brady.

Am I really going to do this?

She scooted further down the row and put a hand on her mother's knee. "Mom. Dad. I'm staying in Ashnee Valley."

I guess I am.

She sat on the floor, whipped off her shoes and flung them behind her.

"Here we go!" she announced when back up on her knees. Scooting faster, she pumped her arms like a locomotive, yucking it up for the audience that was fully engaged in the drama she created. People beyond the front row stood peering over Ben and her parents' shoulders to see.

"You're staying?" Ben said when she reached him.

"Yes. I mean, it depends. You're not the only one with a proposal tonight." She laughed and waved her hands. "Stop!" she said to the crowd chattering wildly and catching on to what she was about to do.

Ben scooted his chair back and lowered to his knees. "So, this is how we're doing this?"

"Ben. Get up. Seriously."

"Nope. I want to be face to face, heart to heart."

Slipping her arms around his neck, Catherine launched forward, her eyes as wide as his when he tipped sideways and landed on his bottom with her in his arms.

"You're going to marry me!"

"Was that a question?" He grinned. "Because it seemed more like a statement."

"It was supposed to be a proposal with me down on one knee. But now we're rolling around the floor together in front of my parents and the whole town."

"I'm sorry."

"Shush. You are not." Still sprawled over Ben, she raised herself on one arm and pointed to the crowd. "Now listen, all of you. It's winter so I can't climb Dragonfly Hill to do this the Ashnee Valley way, no matter how romantic the notion. Besides, I'm forty years old and now my knees are killing me."

"I thought you were thirty-seven?"

"You're missing the point, Ben." Catherine twisted in his arms and gestured toward the tree. "Lucy, hit the lights."

"How many people are in on this?" Ben asked as the room went dark and the Christmas tree sparkled.

"Ben Mannis. I hung two hundred dragonfly ornaments on this tree. Or rather, Ray and others did. My cousin Rodney is going to run Kendall Publishing so the family business stays in the family." She glanced at her father's grimace when her mother elbowed him in the side. "I bought this lodge. And I love you. Will you marry me?"

"Wait!" Lucy shouted running forward. "We forgot something."

"Seriously. Now?" Catherine joked. "This isn't even the part where we ask if anyone objects. Can Ben just say yes first, before I faint?"

"Hurry up." Ben circled his finger at Lucy. "I want to get a few words in here too."

"Hold your horses." Lucy stood directly in front of Catherine's father. "The whole town knows this sculpture is a gift to the Wheelers and Ashnee Valley. But we also learned there was an expectation it would be purchased. So everyone here contributed and a lot more people who couldn't come tonight. It isn't exactly the ten thousand." Lucy handed an envelope to William Kendall. "The truth is we ended up with a little over twelve thousand dollars."

Catherine let Ben help her to her feet.

"Steady." Ben winked, his hands on her waist.

"Did you do this too?"

"I had no idea this part was in the works. Catherine, I never thought I'd get a second chance after you left. I don't want to miss out on my life any more, on *our* lives. What I want is for you to have all your great loves. To experience all your passions. Your life as an artist. Children, if you want. And well, me, of course."

Ben took her hands and lowered to one knee. "You were wrong about us when we first met.

We may be late bloomers, but not reluctant. I was wrong for thinking love has a timeline. I want to claim what we have together and share it for as long as we can. What I'm trying to say is… I accept your proposal, honey. I love you so much. I can't wait to be married to you."

Epilogue

9 years later

BEN KNEW BETTER THAN TO question one of Catherine's sculptures in progress.

Is that a horse? A cow? Whatever it was, it sure had a big belly.

He'd stopped by the lodge early Sunday morning to see if his beloved wife wanted him to include enough scrambled eggs for her too. She hadn't come home the night before. Not that he wasn't used to this by now. She often slept on the old cot at the lodge if she was working until the wee hours of the morning.

He looked at the woman he loved, asleep. Blonde hair strewn across her pillow. Beautiful as an angel. Snoring like a drunken lumberjack.

"Catherine? Are you coming home for breakfast?"

She mashed her face into the pillow. "I'm asleep."

"Would you rather I bring lunch to you later?"

"No. I've been asleep since seven-thirty last night and I'm starving."

He chuckled and sat on the edge of the cot. "Why didn't you call me? I would have picked you up."

She shook her head under the pillow. "Ben, I'm forty-four."

"It's never been entirely clear what your age is."

Catherine pulled the pillow from her face and stuck out her tongue. "We're going to have to get serious. Clean this place up. I don't know." She waved dismissively. "Add carpet or something."

"Carpet?" He lifted her hand and studied the clay caked under her fingernails. "And why's that, sweetheart? I like this place."

"You do not."

He fell back on the bed laughing when she mashed her pillow into his face. Scooting up he snuggled next to her. "This place is you," he said, kissing behind her ear in the way he knew made her crazy. "I like you. All messy sexy." He rose on his elbow and wiggled his eyebrows. "Want to get it on?"

"This is exactly why we need carpet."

"Sounds like rug burn to me. I prefer the bed."

"Ben."

He ran his hand up the inside of her thigh. "Yes, dear."

Catherine grabbed his face with both hands and burst into tears.

"Okay, that's not the first time you've done that, but it still scares the crap out of me."

Her chin quivered. "I have to eat a lot of eggs.

And I have to drink milk. And I can't stay up every night sculpting. I mean, I'll be up all night, that's for sure."

"Aw, honey. I think we both know what's going on. Do you want me to say it, or do you?"

She closed her eyes with a groan. "Number three."

He kissed the salty tears from her cheek. "You know I'll be a hundred when this kid is in college. Is it a sister or brother for Kai and James?

"A boy."

"You've guessed right every time."

She sat up and pointed at the big bellied beast across the room. "It's obvious after all."

Best to agree.

"Ah, I see it."

"See what, Ben? That's just a ridiculously overweight cow."

"Of course."

"No. I had a dream last night, and it's a boy who moves like the wind is chasing him. We're naming him Jett."

"Yeah, so he's fast?"

"Sometimes too fast. Wild. He's going to give Kai and James a run for their money. And you too, Ben."

He caught a glimpse of sadness in her eyes. The usual melancholy of his sweet artist wife.

Ben lay back on the bed and looked at the ceiling. "Kai soft like water. James solid as rock. Jett wild as the wind." Gently, he pulled Catherine down next to him, lying face to face, his hand on her hip.

"Me and my silly dreams."

"Never silly." He tucked her hair behind her ear and brushed her cheek with his thumb. "God, I love you Catherine and I love our life together."

"I love you too, Ben. I want to dance with you and our kids in the sunshine. After breakfast, let's hike Dragonfly Hill."

"Sounds like a perfect day."

Acknowledgements

I wanted an editor who I'd learn from and I couldn't have asked for a better experience. Thank you, Barbara Bettis for editing *Dragonfly Dance*. I love the book covers designed by Kim Killion. So beautiful. I can't wait for readers to see covers for the whole series. For proofreading and answering my many questions with expertise and grace, thank you Jennifer Jakes.

Laurie Cooper and Pub-Craft, bring the professional and polish to my website, social media and promotion. Thank you for your collaboration and support.

To my talented critique partners, C.K. Alber, Dawn Annis, Lori Corsentino, Mary Hagen and Tina Newcomb, thank you for your generosity. I am inspired by each of you and cherish our friendships.

Most important, to my husband and son, thank you for your love and encouragement.

Also By Becca Maxton

MERCY MOUNTAIN SERIES
Dragonfly Dance

Dragonfly Dance was only the beginning. Let's leap ahead a few years, shall we?
The Mannis Family offspring are all grown up & ready for their own detours to romance.

COMING NEXT!
Firefly Duet
Honeybee Rhythm
Butterfly Song

For sneak peeks and the latest release dates sign up for my newsletter at
www.beccamaxton.com

About the Author

Becca Maxton is a contemporary romance author. She writes sensuous (dare say, steamy) and encouraging stories about rocky road detours leading to resilience and romance. Her characters are brave women and men facing challenges together and finding love. Becca is a member of Romance Writers of America, Colorado Romance Writers and the best critique group of writer friends ever. She lives in Colorado with her husband and son.

Follow Becca Maxton on Facebook
and Instagram
@BeccaMaxtonAuthor
or visit *www.beccamaxton.com*.
She enjoys meeting and connecting
with readers online.

Manufactured by Amazon.ca
Acheson, AB